Wildflowers

Dr. Sulagna Mohanty

Shubhapallaba
Publication

WILDFLOWERS

By: Dr. Sulagna Mohanty

Published by:
Shubhapallaba Publication
Email: publication@shubhapallaba.in
Contact: +91 7008899643

Availble at:
Shubhapallaba Store
Amazon India, Flipkart
Typeset Design: Sangram Keshari Senapati
Font: Times New Roman (12 points, text)

ISBN: 978-81-962065-4-3
First impression January 2025

Printed at Shubhodaya Press, Bhadrak, Odisha

Dedicated to

ALL THE WOMEN
IN LOVE

Prologue

A Rural Village of Odisha, the 70s

The small village was always a peaceful place, nestled amidst rolling hills and lush green fields. The wildflowers in the village were a sight to behold, with a vast array of colours spreading across the fields. The bright yellow of the sunflowers swayed gently in the soft breeze, and the tall stems were dotted with delicate, disc-shaped blooms. The purple wildflowers looked like a beautiful shower of rain, spreading out in all directions and filling the air with a sweet fragrance. The wild roses in pink and red added a touch of romance to the fields, with their petals soft and velvety to the touch. As the village girls played on the ground with the flowers, the colours danced around him, creating a whimsical and magical world filled with joy and beauty. The village was transformed into a fairy tale world, where the colours of nature, the soft rustle of the flowers, and the warm sunbeams all combined to create a dreamlike atmosphere.

But on this fateful day, the serenity was shattered by a scene of horror. A young girl, no more than ten, stood frozen with fear, watching in disbelief as two women were beaten to death in the village square. The women were surrounded by an angry mob, their voices raised in a chorus of condemnation, their fists raised in fury.

The small girl could not make out what they were shouting, for the only sound that filled her ears was the music of fear. She watched, helpless and horrified, as the two women were dragged away and locked in a room. The sounds of their screams echoed in the small girl's mind as she tried to make sense of what she was witnessing.

As the hours passed, the small girl grew brave enough to peer into the room where the women were being held. Through a tiny peephole, she saw them lying there, their bodies battered and broken, their spirits crushed. She saw one of the women weakly lift her hand, as if trying to reach out for help, before letting it fall back to her side.

Just as the small girl was about to turn away, a hand patted her shoulder, causing her to jump in fear. She spun around in fear.

She had realized that this small village, once so peaceful and harmonious, was now torn apart by hate and violence. This was the beginning of a journey that would test her courage and her convictions. A journey that would lead her to uncover the ugliness behind the violence that had overtaken their village, and to learn that the price of deception can be far greater than anyone could ever imagine.

Contents

Chapter 1: The Inception

1

The same village, the 90s

Mala's eyes fluttered open, the memories of that fateful day still fresh in her mind, even after all these years. She rubbed the sleep from her eyes and listened as her mother's voice called out to her, reminding her that it was late in the morning and they needed to go to the zamindar Mr Ray's house to help out.

"Come on, Mala, get up," her mother Ketaki said, her voice tinged with urgency. "We have to go to Mr Ray's house. They have guests and Mrs Ray needs our help in the kitchen."

Mala sighed and got up from her bed, her mind still caught up in the past. She shook her head, trying to dispel the memories and focus on the present. As she got dressed, she couldn't help but wonder how much the village had changed since that fateful day.

As she and Ketaki made their way to Mr Ray's house, Mala couldn't help but be struck by the beauty of the village. The sun was shining down on the fields, casting a warm golden glow on the green fields and the people working in them. The sound of laughter and conversation filled the air, and the village was alive with the hum of activity.

But as they approached Mr Ray's house, the mood changed. The air was thick with the smell of cooking food, and the sounds of laughter and conversation were replaced by the clanging of pots and pans. Mr Ray's wife was in the kitchen, working tirelessly to feed the guests who had come to visit.

Ketaki made her way to the kitchen to help out, leaving Mala to wander the grounds. As she walked, she couldn't help but think about the nightmare which once was a truth. The peace in her mind had been replaced by a sense of unease as if something was lurking just beneath the surface.

2

As she stumbled down the lonely corridor, Mala felt her heart pounding against her chest. The familiar gaze of Santosh, the son of the wealthy zamindar Mr Ray, made her skin crawl. She had faced this situation too many times before and knew what he wanted.

"Please, leave me alone," she whispered, trying to back away from his grasp.

But Santosh was relentless, his greedy eyes fixed on her as he reached out to grab her hand. Mala felt a surge of fear and desperation, and she knew she had to escape. She turned and ran, her slender legs carrying her as fast as they could go.

Outside, she breathed in the fresh air, grateful to be free from the suffocating atmosphere of the zamindar's home. She looked up at the sky, dotted with puffy white clouds, and felt a glimmer of hope.

As Mala walked down the rural road, her thoughts

were clouded with the events of the day. She was still shaken by the encounter with Santosh, and her mind kept going back to that moment when his hand reached out to grab hers. She took a deep breath and tried to shake off the feeling of disgust that had taken root in her heart. She didn't want to let the actions of one person control her emotions.

As she walked, she felt a nagging feeling of being followed. She glanced over her shoulder to see a man on a bicycle, pedalling slowly behind her. She recognized him instantly as Mohan, a boy she had known since childhood. Despite his innocence, Mohan usually followed her from a distance though he had never shared his feelings. But today, something was different. Mala's smile was wistful as she remembered how he would always look away whenever their eyes met.

Mala reached her home and looked back to see Mohan disappearing into the distance, still on his bicycle. She couldn't help but feel a sense of longing for something she couldn't quite put her finger on. Perhaps it was a sign of things to come, she thought, as she entered her home and went about her day, waiting for the next chapter in her life to unfold.

3

As the door creaked open, Mala was jolted out of her happy reverie, her heart skipping a beat. The letters, tied neatly in a green cloth, seemed to mock her as she quickly tucked them away, hiding them from the piercing gaze of her mother.

"Mala! How many times have I told you to keep the door closed? Do you have no sense at all? You're not a child anymore," scolded Ketaki, as she bustled into the room.

Mala hung her head in shame, feeling like a scolded child all over again. She couldn't bear to see the disappointment in her mother's eyes, but at the same time, she knew that the letters were a part of her, a part of her happiness and dream that she refused to let go.

"I'm sorry, Maa," mumbled Mala, as she busied herself with tidying up the kitchen, hoping to distract her mother from the letters.

"You must be more careful, Mala. We can't afford to be careless, especially with all the danger lurking around us," warned Ketaki, her voice softening as she hugged her daughter.

Mala hugged her mother back, feeling a sense of comfort and safety in her embrace. She knew that her mother only had her best interests at heart and she couldn't bear to hurt her. But at the same time, she couldn't bear to let go of the letters and the happiness they brought her.

As the mother and daughter went about their chores, Mala's mind wandered, pondering over Mohan who had been following her and the letters that held the key to her happiness. Little did she know that the journey ahead was filled with obstacles, heartache, and triumph and that the letters and the man were intricately woven into the fabric of her destiny.

4

Mala looked down at her plate, her thoughts elsewhere. Suddenly, her mother's voice brought her back to reality.

"Mala, I have some news for you," said Ketaki, wiping her hands on her saree. "There are two proposals for you."

Mala's heart sank. She knew what was coming next.

"Mohan's mother came to see me today. She was asking if you would consider marrying Mohan. You know, every day he comes after you, dragging his cycle. The whole village knows he likes you, and everyone knows he's poor."

"Maa, I don't want to get married," replied Mala, her voice barely above a whisper.

"Well, you have to consider these proposals," said Ketaki, her tone firm. "The second proposal is from a widower in Bhawanipur who has a saree shop. He's richer than any of the other prospective grooms I've seen."

Mala sighed. She knew her mother meant well, but the thought of getting married to someone she didn't love filled her with dread.

"I'm not interested in getting married to anyone, Maa," said Mala, getting up from the table. "I'll do the dishes."

"At least take your dishes," Ketaki snapped. "I'm not your servant. I'll see who will take your plate in your in-laws' house."

Mala sighed again, taking the dishes to the sink. She couldn't help but think about the life that was being planned for her, a life she wasn't sure she wanted.

The mother's words echoed in Mala's head as she walks to the washbasin, her steps heavy with the weight of society's expectations. Her heart aches with the thought of being wed to a man, leaving behind the only home she's ever known and living a life of servitude under the thumb of a man she's never met. The water cascades over her hands as she washes away the remnants of the meal, but she knows that the thoughts of the marriage proposals will not be so easily washed away.

She dries her hands and turns to face her mother, the

anger and defiance evident in her eyes. "I will not be a mere possession to be traded for wealth or status," she declares, her voice firm and resolute. "I will not spend my life being told what to do, who to love, and how to live."

Ketaki scoffs, "Who will want you if you do not agree to these proposals? You are a grown woman; it is time for you to be married and start a family of your own."

"I will make my own way in the world," replies Mala, her voice rising.

Ketaki huffs and returns to her meal, dismissing her daughter's protests as the fanciful dreams of a young girl. But deep down, Mala knows that she must fight for her own happiness, even if it means defying the expectations of those around her. And so, she begins a journey of self-discovery, determined to forge her own path in a world that seems intent on holding her back.

5

Mala walked through the village with a sense of purpose, her feet pounding the dusty earth with each step. The sun was high in the sky and the heat was relentless, but she paid it no mind. Her thoughts were consumed by the recent proposal she had received, and the weight of the decision she now carried with her.

As she approached the temple, she saw Mohan waiting for her, his bicycle resting against a tree. Mala's heart sank as she realized what was about to happen. She tried to steel herself for the conversation ahead, but the words still caught in her throat as Mohan approached her.

"Mala, I hope you've had a chance to think about my proposal," Mohan said, his voice eager and nervous all at once.

Mala took a deep breath and looked directly into Mohan's eyes. "I have, Mohan," she said, her voice steady and calm. "And I will tell my mother my decision when the time is right. You need not worry about it."

Mohan's face fell, but he quickly regained his composure. "I understand," he said. "Just know that I am here, waiting, whenever you are ready to give me your answer."

And with that, Mohan turned and mounted his bicycle, pedalling away into the distance. Mala watched him go, a mix of emotions swirling within her. She knew that the road ahead was uncertain, but she was determined to make the best decision for herself, no matter the outcome.

6

The moonlight cascaded through the window, illuminating the room with a soft silver glow. The stillness of the night was only interrupted by the sound of quiet breathing. But as the moon rose higher in the sky, the peace was broken by the mother's voice.

"Mala, my dear, have you made a decision about the proposals?" the mother asked softly.

Mala's eyes fluttered open, and she turned to face her mother. "Yes, Ma. I have made up my mind," she replied, her voice steady and resolute.

Ketaki's eyebrows shot up in surprise. "Really? And who have you chosen?" she asked.

"I have decided to marry the widower from Bhawanipur," Mala said, her voice ringing with confidence.

Ketaki let out a sigh, her hand coming up to massage

her temples. “Are you sure, Mala? He is a widower, you know. It is not easy to be a second wife.”

“I am aware of that, Maa. But I have made up my mind,” Mala replied, determination in her voice.

Ketaki looked at Mala, a mixture of surprise and pride in her eyes. “Well, if this is what you have decided, then so be it. But remember, you must be strong and brave in your new life.”

Mala nodded, a small smile playing on her lips. And with that, she closed her eyes, ready to face whatever the future held for her. The moon shone down on her, casting a soft light on her peaceful face as if to bless her journey ahead.

Chapter 2: A New Beginning

7

The day had finally arrived. The sun rose over the small village, casting its warm glow over the quaint homes and bustling streets. The sounds of clanging pots and chanting prayers filled the air, as preparations for the wedding of Mala and Sharad were underway.

Mala sat in her room, dressed in a beautiful red saree with gold accents. She looked ethereal, a vision of grace and beauty. Ketaki, stood by her side, her eyes misty with tears. It was a bittersweet moment for both of them, as Mala was about to embark on a new journey, leaving behind the only home she had ever known.

"Are you sure you're ready for this?" asked Ketaki, her voice trembling with emotion.

Mala simply nodded; her eyes fixed on the door. She had made her decision, and there was no turning back now.

The wedding was a simple affair, steeped in tradition and sanctity. The villagers had gathered in the open courtyard, dressed in their finest clothes and adorned with flowers. The air was heavy with the scent of incense, as prayers were offered and vows were exchanged and of course, Mohan was nowhere to be seen.

As the ceremony came to an end, Mala was bid farewell

by her mother and the rest of the village. Tears flowed freely, as people hugged her and wished her all the best for her future.

Mala climbed onto the back of Sharad's rented car, and they rode off into the horizon, leaving behind the only home she had ever known. The villagers watched in silence, as the bicycle grew smaller and smaller until it finally disappeared from sight.

"Farewell, my love," whispered Ketaki, as the tears continued to flow down her face. "May you find happiness and love in your new home?"

8

As Mala sat in her first night room, her heart pounded with nervousness and fear. She felt like a bird trapped in a cage, longing to take flight but unable to do so. The door creaked open and in stepped her husband, Sharad. The room was filled with intense silence as the two of them locked eyes. Mala wanted to speak, to express her fears and reservations, but the words seemed to get stuck in her throat.

Sharad moved closer, his hand tenderly caressing her face. Mala was both scared and shy, her mind grappling with the strange new feelings that were coursing through her body.

The room was lit only by the soft glow of the moon, casting a mystical aura over the scene. It was as if time had frozen, and the world was holding its breath, waiting to see what would happen next. The room was filled with an aura of mystery as if it held a secret that only the two of them were privy to.

At that moment, Mala felt a spark of fear ignites

within her heart. She felt like she was about to embark on a treacherous journey, one that would lead her into dangerous unknowns and force her to face the hardships of life in ways she had never encountered before. And as she looked into the eyes of her husband, she felt a shiver run down her spine, a feeling of dread and uncertainty, unsure if she was ready to take the first step into the unknown.

The door was closed. The night was silent but then the silence of the night was stirred by a painful cry.

Mala's world had come crashing down. She felt like she was falling into an endless pit, surrounded by darkness and fear. The cuts and bites on her face were a painful reminder of the fate that had befallen her and something she had chosen for herself. She couldn't help but let the tears flow down her cheeks. She was dishevelled, her hair and kohl smudged, and her sindoor in disarray, reflecting the turmoil that was raging within her. The pain was palpable, and as she sat on the floor, she felt like she had lost everything she had ever held dear. The future looked bleak, and she wondered if she would ever find her way back to the light. But then why did it feel that her eyes were hiding something?

9

As the sun shone brightly in the sky, little Mala laughed and played in the garden. Her joyous spirit was contagious as she ran around with abandon, her laughter ringing through the air like the peals of a bell. The sound of footsteps could be heard, running behind her, following closely in pursuit. Mala was caught up in the moment, lost in the pure, unbridled joy of childhood. As she looked up to the sky, she was filled with a sense of wonder and hope, as if the world was full of endless possibilities. And at this moment, she was free, without a care in the world, lost in the beauty of life.

As the sun shone brightly in the sky, Mala came back to her present. She had stood in the courtyard, taking down clothes from the line. Her scars, the visible remnants of the torture she endured daily, were a testament to the pain she carried with her. With every movement, she was reminded of the wounds that marred her face, hands, and neck. As she brought the clothes to her room, she couldn't help but remember the carefree days of her childhood.

She placed the clothes on the shelf and opened her almirah, taking out the gift she had always kept close to her. With a soft touch, she took it in her hand and gazed at it, lost in thought. But before she could fully absorb the memories it evoked; her mother-in-law Ambika's voice shattered the silence.

"Mala! Where are you? I need your help in the kitchen," Ambika called out, breaking Mala's reverie. Quickly, she placed the object back in the drawer and hastened to her mother-in-law's side, leaving behind the memories and the mystery of what lay hidden in her almirah.

10

As Sharad enters the room, still damp from his morning bath, he begins to get ready for his day at the shop. But as he searches for his beloved watch, a look of frustration clouds his face. He rips apart the bed sheets and scours every nook and cranny of the room, but the watch remains elusive. Just as he begins to rummage through the drawers, Mala enters the room, her heart beating wildly in her chest. She fears that the precious gift she had hidden in the drawer will be discovered by her husband.

But to her relief, Sharad finds only his watch and slips it onto his wrist, a relieved smile spreading across his face. As he begins to leave the room, Mala musters up the courage to ask if they can go visit her mother's house. Sharad, barely paying attention, nonchalantly replies, "Ok, ok. We'll see." And with that, he sets off for his shop, leaving Mala alone in the room.

Trembling with fear, Mala cautiously opens the drawer and retrieves the gift, tucking it safely away in the almirah, hidden from prying eyes. She takes a deep breath, steeling herself for another day in this trying marriage, but with a glimmer of hope in her heart, knowing that she has something to hold onto, something that gives her a small measure of comfort.

11

As Mala worked alongside her mother-in-law in the courtyard, the sun shining down on their shared task, she couldn't help but be drawn to a corner shelf filled with hairpins. Her fingers reached out and plucked one from its resting place, the smooth metal warm from the sun's rays. And then she saw it - a saree box, tucked away in the corner, calling out to her with its promise of something beautiful.

She cast a quick glance over her shoulder, making sure no one was watching, and lifted the lid of the box. What she found inside took her breath away - sarees of all colours, patterns, and textures. Her eyes were immediately drawn to one, a vibrant shade of green, with delicate golden threads woven through it. She knew she had to have it.

But as she stepped out of the room, wearing the new saree, Ambika's horrified reaction caught her off guard. "Take it off, take it off!" the older woman cried, "That belongs to Sharad's dead wife, Laxmi!"

Mala's heart sank as she looked at Ambika's face, filled with shock and disbelief. "What do you mean, it belongs to Laxmi?" she asked, trying to make sense of the situation.

"That saree, it was Laxmi's favourite," the older woman explained, her voice shaking. "She wore it on special occasions, it holds a lot of sentimental value for Sharad. You can't wear it, it's disrespectful."

Mala's hand instinctively went to the fabric of the saree, feeling the smoothness of the silk under her fingers. She hadn't meant to cause any offence; she had simply been drawn to the beauty of the saree and wanted to try it on.

"I'm so sorry," she said, feeling a knot form in her throat. "I didn't know. I found it in the storeroom and I liked it, I thought it would be okay to wear it."

Ambika took a deep breath and placed a hand on her shoulder. "It's alright," she said, her voice softening. "Just go take it off and we'll forget about this. We don't want to upset Sharad."

Mala nodded, feeling a wave of regret wash over her. She had always been careful to avoid upsetting her mother-in-law or Sharad, but it seemed like she couldn't do anything right. As she went back to her room to change, she couldn't shake the feeling that she was always one step away from making a mistake in this new family she had married into.

She had heard of Laxmi before, but the name alone filled her with a sense of unease. She quickly retreated back to her room, her mind racing as she struggled to understand what was happening. As she removed the beautiful saree, she couldn't help but feel a sense of loss, as if she had been deprived of something special that was never meant for her to have. And she couldn't shake the feeling that Laxmi was watching her, reminding her that she was just a newcomer in this household, and there were still so many secrets waiting to be uncovered.

That evening, Sharad arrived home drunk and stormed into the room. Pretending to be asleep, Mala was jolted awake as her husband roughly pulled her up. Despite resisting, she was slapped harshly, causing her to fall to the floor. With a swift kick from Sharad, Mala cried out in pain as her saree was tossed aside, landing on the ground.

Chapter 3: Mother's Home

12

Ketaki sat on the veranda with Mohan's mother Rajni, her eyes staring blankly into the distance. The sun was setting and the sky was painted in hues of orange and pink, but her mind was far from the beauty around her. Rajni's words had brought up memories of the past and she was lost in thought.

"So finally, they are visiting you," Rajni spoke up, breaking the silence. "It's already six months since their wedding and they still haven't come to see you. Although my son may not be wealthy, I wish you had agreed to the proposal. At least your daughter would have been under your roof."

Ketaki sighed, "I came to know about all these things far too late. I am just a poor widow, who would have told me?"

Rajni nodded sympathetically, "I heard it from my neighbour. After Mala's marriage, a friend from Sharad's village told her about the rumours surrounding Sharad's first wife Laxmi. People still don't know if it was an accident or something more sinister."

Ketaki shook her head, "It's too late now, anyway. Mala made her choice and married Sharad. Now her fate is in her own hands."

Rajni then asked, "And what about Mohan's wedding? Has he found a bride yet?"

Ketaki frowned, "You know about the land dispute with Mohan's uncle, elder brother of my late husband. Until that is resolved, we cannot inherit any of our ancestral property. In such circumstances, who would want to marry into our family?"

Rajni shrugged, "Even you turned down his proposal. But it's fine. I'll send over some pancakes for Mala, she loves them." With a smile, Rajni got up to leave, leaving Ketaki alone with her thoughts once again.

As she sat there, Ketaki couldn't help but feel a sense of unease. The rumours surrounding Sharad and his first wife lingered in her mind, and she couldn't shake off the feeling that her daughter may be in danger. The pancakes may bring a temporary smile to her daughter's face, but Ketaki feared what the future may hold for her.

13

As Mohan sat on the veranda of Mala's home, he felt his heart weigh heavy with a mixture of sadness and anger. The sight of his childhood friend, now married to a man he clearly detested, was almost too much for him to bear. Mohan was a man of few words, but the feelings he held within him spoke volumes. He sat there on the veranda, silently observing the interactions between Mala and her husband, Sharad. The once bubbly and carefree Mala had transformed into a woman who seemed lost, her eyes carrying the weight of the world.

When the introduction was made by Ketaki, he could see the disdain in Sharad's eyes and the way he mockingly looked at Mala. Maybe he was aware of Mohan's proposal for Mala. "Yes, I have heard a lot about him…," said Sharad and giving a smirk.

Mohan was already feeling frustrated at Sharad's lack of respect, but this comment was the final straw. He could feel his anger boiling within him as Sharad's condescending tone and sarcastic smirk grated on his nerves.

Mohan stood up abruptly, his fists clenched at his sides, trying to rein in his emotions. He didn't want to create a scene in front of Mala's mother, but it was becoming increasingly difficult. His anger boiled over and he stood up, the chair scraping against the floor in his haste to leave. "I must be going," he said curtly, unable to hide the rage in his voice. He felt his fists clench as he started to walk away, the image of Sharad's contemptuous smile still burning in his mind.

He shot a quick, apologetic look at Ketaki before turning on his heel and storming out of the house, not even bothering to say goodbye. He could feel Sharad's mocking gaze following him as he walked out, but he refused to look back.

As he walked down the road, Mohan took a deep breath and tried to calm down. He was filled with a mixture of sadness and anger as he thought about what had just happened. He had always hoped that one day, Mala would come to her senses and realize that he was the one for her. But now, seeing her with Sharad, he was forced to face the harsh reality that his dreams were never going to come true.

He trudged back to his house and his mother could see the turmoil in his eyes she hugged him tightly, offering comfort and understanding. "It will all work out in the end, my son," she whispered, "just trust in the universe and have faith."

Mohan nodded, but he couldn't shake the feeling that everything was falling apart. He tried to push away the sadness that threatened to engulf him. He knew that he had to be strong for himself, and for the memories of the life he had dreamt of sharing with Mala.

14

The room was filled with moonlight filtering through the curtains, painting the room in a silver hue. As Sharad left the house, Ketaki was left with a feeling of disappointment and sadness. She had so hoped for a reunion with her daughter, but it seemed that Sharad was in a hurry to leave and would not stay even for a moment longer.

"What a pity," she thought to herself. "I hoped to catch a glimpse of my daughter's life and see how she has been faring. But it seems that Sharad has other plans."

Mala, however, seemed unfazed by her husband's hasty departure. She was lying alongside her mother with a distant look in her eyes, lost in thought. Ketaki spoke to her cautiously, not wanting to disrupt her thoughts.

"Mala, my dear, are you alright?" she asked softly.

"Yes Maa," replied Mala, snapping out of her reverie. "I just have a lot on my mind.

"Why did Sharad leave so early?"

Mala smiled. "Sharad has been under a lot of pressure lately, with his shop and all. And I worry about him, especially with the added responsibility of finding a new assistant," she replied.

Her mother nodded understandingly. "I understand, my child. It's hard to manage a business and keep everything running smoothly. But, tell me, is everything else alright between the two of you? I sense a hint of sadness in your eyes."

Mala hesitated for a moment, then looked at her mother with a faint smile. "We're fine, Maa. It's just the usual stresses of married life."

Ketaki's hand felt warm on Mala's belly, a gesture of comfort and love. "How many months is it?" Ketaki's asked in a soft voice.

"Three months," Mala replied, her voice barely above a whisper. Ketaki's hand tightened around Mala's as she asked, "So are you sure? Are you happy with your new family?"

Mala turned to face the wall, hiding her face from her mother's view. The tears started to flow down her cheeks as she replied, "Yes, I am happy there."

Ketaki caressed and patted her back. "That's all that matters, my dear. As long as you two are happy, everything else will fall into place." She folded her hands and looked towards the heavens, silently thanking the almighty for her daughter's happiness.

Mala lay there, lost in thought, her eyes fixed on the wall. The love and concern of her mother, the comfort of her home, and the uncertainty of her new life all tangled up inside of her, creating a storm of emotions. She knew deep down that she was happy for the baby, but the fear of the unknown and the adjustments to her new life weighed heavily on her heart.

As Mala lay there, surrounded by the love of her mother, she closed her eyes, letting herself be enveloped by the comfort and peace of the moment. She knew that no matter where life took her, the love and support of her family would always be there, guiding her through the storm. And with that, the two of them sat in comfortable silence, enjoying the peace and quiet of the veranda and basking in the warmth of their love for each other.

15

As the small girl made her way home in the dark, fear shrouded her like a cloak. Every rustle of leaves and every creak of a branch made her heart race. She felt so alone, like a small bird lost in the vastness of the sky. Just as she thought she couldn't take it anymore, a ray of light cut through the darkness. She turned to see a small boy, no more than ten years old, walking towards her with a torch.

"Don't be afraid," the boy said with a gentle smile, as he saw the fear in the girl's eyes. "I'll walk with you."

The girl couldn't help but feel a sense of comfort as the boy walked alongside her. With every step, she felt safer and less afraid. She looked up at the boy and saw a warm smile on his face, filled with kindness and reassurance.

Mala still remembered that night and Mohan's kind gesture towards her. She wanted to talk to Mohan that morning. But Mohan was avoiding her, and it was beginning to take a toll on her emotions. Despite her efforts to reach out to him, he seemed distant and uninterested in talking to her. The once warm smile he used to give her was now replaced by an indifferent gaze.

That morning, Mala stood on the road, staring after Mohan as he walked away avoiding her. Mohan seemed distant and cold. Mala felt a pang of sadness in her heart and a small tear escaped from her eye. Though she had a bit idea of what was going on with him, she was determined to talk to him.

She slowly walked over to him and gently placed her hand on his shoulder. "Mohan, what's wrong?" she asked, her voice filled with concern.

Mohan shrugged her hand off and turned to face her, his eyes blazing with anger. "Why do you always have to be so nosy, Mala?

Can't you just mind your own business?" he snapped.

Mala was taken aback by his sudden outburst. She had never seen Mohan behave like this before. "I'm just worried about you, Mohan," she said softly.

Mohan looked away, his expression softening. "I'm sorry, Mala. I didn't mean to snap at you. It's just that... that I don't want to talk to you right now."

Mohan's heart was heavy with the weight of unrequited love. Yet, Mohan refused to let his emotions consume him and cause chaos in her life. Instead, he made the difficult decision to distance himself from her, to spare her any discomfort or embarrassment.

Mala looked at him with understanding, her heart overflowing with love and compassion for this poor man. "It's okay, Mohan," says Mala softly. I understand you."

Mohan sighed and left. Mala felt a pang of sadness in her heart. She had always known Mohan to be a kind soul, someone who was always there for her in good times and bad. As she stood there, lost in her thoughts, she couldn't help but feel a twinge of regret for the way things had turned out between them. But she knew that there was nothing she could do to change it.

Chapter 4: The Uninvited Guest

16

"Sir Namaste," the young woman said, her voice ringing like a clear bell on a still night. Sharad looked up from his calculations, surprise evident on his face as he took in the sight before him.

She was a vision, with hair as black as a moonless sky and eyes as bright as stars. She stood there, a ray of light in the otherwise dim and dreary shop.

"I am Chandra," she said, her voice soft and musical. For a moment, Sharad was at a loss for words. He had never seen such beauty before, and it was as if all the words in the world had deserted him.

But then, he composed himself and stood up from his chair, a smile spreading across his face. "Namaste," he said. "What brings you here?"

"I am looking for a job," Chandra said, her voice steady and confident. "I heard that you need an assistant and I thought I could help."

Sharad looked at her, his eyebrows raised in surprise. "You want to work in an electronic shop?" he asked a hint of amusement in his voice.

"Yes," Chandra replied, her eyes shining with

determination. "I may not have much experience, but I am a fast learner and I am willing to do whatever it takes to succeed."

Sharad was impressed by her tenacity and he could see that she would be a valuable asset to his business. So, he hired her on the spot and just in a day she became a familiar face in the shop, her laughter ringing out like music every time a customer walked in.

And so, that day Sharad's little electronic shop was transformed by the light of Chandra's smile and the customers came drawn by her beauty and the quality of the product on sale. Sharad couldn't have been happier with his new assistant, and he was grateful for the chance to encounter that had brought her into his life that day.

17

Ketaki smiled at Rajni as she walked into their small home. "It's been two months," Rajni said, concern etched on her face. "Why hasn't Sharad come to take Mala yet?"

"In our caste, the first child is always born in the father-in-law's place," Ketaki explained. "But I'm not sure why Sharad hasn't come. I'll send him a message."

Rajni nodded and then brought the good news of her own. "Our property case has finally been solved. We're going to sell the land, and Mohan is opening a small jewellery workshop. He's a goldsmith by profession, after all."

Ketaki's face lit up at the news. "That's wonderful! I'm so happy for Mohan." Just then, Mala walked in from the shop, her baby bump now more noticeable. "What's the good news?" she asked, a smile on her face.

"Mohan is opening a jewellery workshop," Ketaki said,

beaming with pride.

Mala's face lit up as well. "That's wonderful news. Congratulations!"

Rajni smiled warmly. "We would love for you to join us for dinner today. After all, you're carrying a little one inside of you."

Mala agreed, and the three women sat down to a warm, delicious meal together, surrounded by love and happiness. The future looked bright for all of them, and they were grateful for each other's support and friendship.

18

The dinner was set in Mohan's house, with the warm aroma of home-cooked food filling the air. Rajni and Ketaki sat together, chatting and laughing while they prepared the food. Mala sat quietly; her eyes fixed on Mohan who was avoiding her gaze. Despite the laughter and merriment, there was an unmistakable aura of unease that surrounded Mohan.

As they began to eat, Ketaki struck up a conversation with Rajni, but Mohan remained silent, only picking at his food. Mala tried to engage him in conversation, but he merely nodded in response, his eyes avoiding hers. The silence between them was palpable, and it was clear that something was weighing heavy on Mohan's heart.

After the dinner, Mala turned to Ketaki and Rajni and listened as Rajni talked excitedly about finalizing a bride for her son. Mala, in a fit of joy, turned to Mohan to offer her congratulations who had moved to the drawing room. But the smile on her face quickly faded as she saw the coldness in Mohan's eyes.

Mala hesitantly approached Mohan and asked, "Are

you still angry with me?"

Mohan looked at her, his eyes dark with emotion, "As if you don't know, Mala."

Mala's heart went out to Mohan, and she could see the pain in his eyes. "I'm so sorry, Mohan," she said softly. "I never meant to hurt you." Her voice was filled with agony, "The whole world may misunderstand me, Mohan, but not you. You know me better than anyone." But Mohan's reply was as cold as ice, "There's nothing left to understand."

He then turned and walked away, leaving a heartbroken Mala behind. Mala's heart felt as though it had been crushed into a million pieces. But she could understand why Mohan was so distant and why he wouldn't talk to her. She sighed. The once warm and comforting presence of her kind well-wisher friend was now a distant memory.

19

It was a cold, cosy evening in Sharad's village. As Mala and Sharad arrived at their home, the sound of the bike faded into the silence of the evening. Sharad quickly dismounted and helped the pregnant Mala down. This gesture was quite new for Mala. Then he started to leave for his shop.

"Wait, you're not coming for dinner?" Mala asked, surprised by his sudden departure.

"I've got a lot to do today," Sharad replied without looking at her.

Mala watched as he walked away, feeling a twinge of confusion. She had grown used to spending her days without Sharad, but now she was wondering how to face the unknown territory of his family's house alone.

As she walked inside, she was greeted by Ambika. The

older woman's eyes lingered on her for a moment before she spoke.

"Why were you so late in coming back?" Ambika asked her tone a mixture of concern and reproach.

"It was Sharad who didn't go earlier to fetch me home," Mala replied, trying to keep her voice calm and even. "Otherwise, I would have come back sooner."

Ambika shook her head, her disappointment palpable. "I asked Sharad so many times to bring you back, but he always said he was busy," she said, frustration creeping into her voice.

Mala didn't respond, not sure how to respond. Instead, she excused herself and headed to her room to rest. She needed time to process the strange and unsettling feeling that had settled over her since her arrival in Sharad's family's home.

20

It was going to be noon. The sun was shining through the window, and the birds were chirping outside. Mala was in the kitchen, helping Ambika in preparing lunch. Ambika was busy chopping vegetables for the curry, while Mala was grinding spices for the masala.

Suddenly, Ambika turned to Mala and said, "Today Sharad can't come home for lunch. I have to send lunch to his shop." She looked a bit worried as if she was carrying the weight of the world on her shoulders.

Mala noticed the concern in Ambika's voice and asked, "What's wrong, maa? Why can't he come home for lunch today?"

Ambika replied, "These days, Sharad rarely comes

home for lunch. I usually send lunch with our neighbour, but today even he has gone to the city. So, I need someone else to take lunch to the shop for Sharad."

Mala thought for a moment and then said, "Don't worry. I will take lunch to the shop for Sharad today." Ambika smiled and thanked Mala for her help.

Together, the two of them finished preparing the lunch and packed it into a basket. Mala put on her shawl and headed out to the shop, ready to deliver the hot, fresh food to her husband.

21

As Mala entered the shop with the lunchbox, she saw a scene that left her flabbergasted. There was Sharad, her husband, who was busy flirting with a girl. The moment they noticed her, the two of them became still and quiet, like two deer caught in the headlights.

Mala walked towards Sharad, who looked a bit uncomfortable to see her. "Why did you come here?" he asked, trying to hide his unease.

"I brought you the lunchbox," Mala replied simply, holding out the box.

Sharad took the lunchbox from her, "Okay, okay." He said, his eyes darting to the other girl in the shop.

Mala's curiosity was piqued, she turned to the girl and looked at her, taking in her features. The girl had a warm smile that lit up her face and eyes that sparkle with mischief. She had an air of confidence about her that catches everyone's attention. She was dressed in a simple salwar suit that complemented her beauty, and her hair was tied back in a neat bun, showcasing her delicate features.

Chandra looked at Mala and her baby bump. Sharad reluctantly introduced the girl, "This is Chandra, she's the new assistant in the shop."

Chandra smiled at Mala, but the latter didn't reciprocate. "I'm leaving now," Mala said curtly, before turning on her heel and walking out of the shop.

As Mala left, Sharad and Chandra resumed their flirting conversation, their voices low and hushed, like two conspirators. But the damage was done, the seed of doubt had been planted in Mala's mind, and she couldn't shake off the feeling of unease that had taken root inside her.

22

Ambika sighed contentedly as Mala rubbed the warm oil into her feet, massaging the knots and aches away. "You know Mala, I missed having you here to take care of me," Ambika said. "These past few months, since you went away, no one has taken such good care of me."

Mala smiled softly, continuing to rub the oil into Ambika's skin. "I'm glad I could be here for you, maa," she replied.

"And speaking of being here," Ambika continued, "what did Sharad say seeing you in the shop?"

Maybe Mala was waiting for this moment. She hesitated for a moment before asking, "For how many days has that girl been working in the shop with Sharad?"

Ambika sighed. "It's been almost three months now. Since you went home. They spend all day in the shop together, and Sharad even comes home late now," she said, concern etched on her face.

Mala remained quiet, her thoughts lost in a sea of worry and confusion. She couldn't shake the image of Sharad flirting with that girl, Chandra, from her mind. She didn't want to jump to any conclusions, but she couldn't ignore the unease in her heart either.

23

As Sharad sat at the dining table, his eyes fixated on the food in front of him. The aroma that filled the room was no longer appealing to him, and he pushed the plate away with a look of disgust. Mala entered the room holding and asked, "What's wrong with the food?"

Sharad's eyes burned with anger as she stood up, his hands balled into fists. He slammed them on the table, making the cutlery rattle, and spat, "How dare you ask me questions?

Sharad came forward and slapped Mala. The bowl fell from her hand and broke the silence of the night. Sharad was going to hit her again when he was pulled by Ambika.

Ambika stood between the two, her hands raised to stop the physical altercation. She could see the anger boiling inside Sharad and the fear in Mala's eyes. She knew she had to intervene before things escalated any further.

"Stop it, Sharad!" Ambika shouted her voice firm and commanding.

"She is carrying your child; do you want her to face the same fate as Laxmi?"

The mention of Laxmi, Sharad's late wife, made him pause. He looked down at Mala, who was cowering in fear, and then back at his mother. The anger slowly dissipated from his eyes, replaced by a look of confusion.

“What are you talking about?” Sharad asked, his voice filled with anger and frustration.

“You know exactly what I’m talking about,” Ambika replied, her voice steady and unwavering. “You can’t treat her like this, not when she’s carrying your child.”

Sharad’s eyes softened as he realized the gravity of the situation. He let out a sigh and looked away, his mind filled with memories of the past.

“Fine,” he said, his voice quiet and defeated. “Go inside, both of you.”

Ambika took Mala by the arm and led her away from Sharad, who stood there, staring off into the distance. He was filled with a mix of emotions, torn between the ghost of the past and the anger he felt towards his mother’s words.

Chapter 5: The Love Blossoms

24

As Mohan inaugurated his small jewellery workshop, the villagers gathered around, eager to see what he had in store. Mohan stood tall and proud, a smile spreading across his face as he welcomed everyone to his new venture. Rajni, beamed with pride beside him, her eyes glistening with joy.

In the crowd, Ketaki, stood with a smile on her face as she admired the intricate designs on display. She complimented Mohan on his talent, and he thanked her graciously. The villagers marvelled at the intricate designs and sparkling diamonds, their eyes wide with wonder.

As the evening progressed, Mohan gave a tour of his workshop, showing everyone the process of how he crafted each piece of jewellery. The villagers were impressed by his skills and asked questions, eager to learn more about the process.

After the tour, Rajni approached Mohan with a proud smile on her face and said, "I always knew you had a passion for jewellery-making, and today I can see that your hard work has paid off." Mohan smiled at his mother, grateful for her support and encouragement.

Ketaki, who was also impressed by Mohan's work, approached him and said, "Your work is beautiful, Mohan.

I am sure it will be a great success." Mohan thanked her for her kind words and said that he hoped to bring a touch of beauty and elegance to the village through his jewellery.

As the evening came to a close, the villagers left the workshop, their minds filled with the beauty of Mohan's creations. The inauguration of the workshop was a memorable event, and everyone was excited to see what other beautiful pieces Mohan would create in the future.

25

As the days passed, Sharad and Chandra's relationship continued to blossom. As Sharad and Chandra spent more time together at the shop, their playful flirting slowly evolved into a full-blown affair. They would often take impromptu trips to nearby fairs or far-off cities on Sharad's bike, simply enjoying each other's company.

During these outings, they would laugh, dance, and steal secret kisses whenever they got the chance. The thrill of being together and doing something forbidden was exhilarating for both of them. They were completely caught up in the moment, not paying any heed to the consequences of their actions.

Despite this, Sharad was still married to Mala. But he never struggled with the guilt of betraying her. He never tried to push his feelings for Chandra aside as she had already taken a hold of his heart. Likewise, Chandra too was completely smitten with Sharad and would have done anything to be with him.

They continued to keep their relationship a secret, but it was only a matter of time before someone found out. So, the rumours started to spread, and some of the people in the village were talking about the affair. Some villagers disapproved and judged Sharad, but others saw it as a forbidden love story and gossiped about it excitedly. But nothing was open. All of it was in murmur.

However, as their relationship progressed, they started to realize the seriousness of the situation. They knew that if they were caught, they could face severe consequences as Sharad was married. But the love and passion they felt for each other were too strong to ignore. They simply couldn't resist each other's allure.

As they continued to flaunt their relationship, Sharad and Chandra were soon consumed by their own desires. They lived in a world of their own, completely disregarding the norms and traditions of their society. The future of their relationship was uncertain, but for now, they were happy and in love.

26

It was a joyous occasion in the village as Mohan got married to this charming girl named Priti. The wedding ceremony was a vibrant affair, with everyone from the village in attendance. The sun shone brightly in the sky and the birds sang in melodious harmony, as if in celebration of the union of two hearts.

Priti was a vision of beauty, dressed in a vibrant red saree and adorned with sparkling jewels. Her eyes were lit up with happiness, and her smile radiated warmth and joy. Mohan, on the other hand, was dapper in his traditional wedding attire, with a red turban on his head and a broad smile on his face.

As they exchanged vows, the air was filled with the sweet fragrance of flowers and the sound of auspicious mantras. The loving aura of the moment was palpable and contagious, spreading joy to all who were present. The wedding ceremony was followed by a grand feast, where the villagers feasted delicious food and danced to the beat of the drums.

The villagers blessed the newlyweds and wished them a lifetime of happiness and love. As the day came to an end, Mohan and Priti were ready to embark on a journey of love and companionship. And with that, Priti thought a new chapter in their lives will begin, filled with love, laughter, and a lifetime of happiness.

27

As Mohan entered the room, Priti's eyes lit up with anticipation and joy. She eagerly welcomed him with a shy smile, and Mohan couldn't help but feel overwhelmed with love and affection for his new bride. He sat down next to her and took her hand in his, their fingers entwining as if they were made for each other.

Mohan leaned in and placed a soft, loving kiss on Priti's cheek, then on her neck, sending shivers down her spine. As he wrapped his arms around her, Priti felt like she was finally home. She held onto him tightly, feeling safe and secure in his embrace.

As the night progressed, Mohan and Priti lost themselves in each other's arms, their hearts beating as one. They shared sweet kisses and whispered loving words, lost in the magic of their first night as husband and wife. The room was filled with the gentle glow of candlelight, and outside, the stars shone brightly in the sky, as if they were shining just for the two of them.

But as they got lost in the moment, Mohan suddenly became restless. He couldn't shake off the memories of his past, and his mind became filled with doubts and fears. Despite his love for Priti, he found himself struggling to fully surrender to their love.

Mohan got up from the bed, and with a heavy heart, put on his kurta and left the room. Priti watched him go, her heart aching for her new husband. But even as he left, she held onto the hope that one day, he would find the strength to let go of his fears and fully embrace the love that they shared.

28

It was a dark night, and Chandra was shrouded in shadows as she stood in the moonlight. The rustling of leaves and the pitter-patter of raindrops filled the air as she furtively handed over a wad of cash to the mysterious figure in front of her. The man was shrouded in a shawl, and his face was obscured in the darkness.

"This is the last time," Chandra said sternly, her voice as sharp as the lightning that illuminated the sky. "You need to find a different source of income; you can't keep relying on me."

The man merely shrugged, his voice low and raspy as he replied, "I need the money, Chandra. You know that."

Chandra sighed; her frustration palpable as she shook her head. "Just make sure no one sees you, alright?"

The man took the money and disappeared into the night, leaving Chandra alone with her thoughts. She looked up at the sky, watching as the storm raged on, and wondered what she had gotten herself into. The sound of the rain was a symphony of sorrow, each droplet a lament for the life she once had, and the life she now lived.

But even as she stood there, drenched to the bone, Chandra knew that she would do whatever it took to protect the ones she loved. She had made a promise to herself, and she was determined to keep it, no matter the cost.

Chapter 6: A New Dawn

29

The night was dark and oppressive, with clouds hanging heavy in the sky, ready to burst forth in a fit of rain. Laxmi huddled in a corner; her eyes red from the tears that wouldn't stop flowing. Sharad stood in front of her, his voice raised in anger as he scolded her for what seemed like hours.

"Today, I will leave you in your father's house and bring a new wife." Sharad's words were like knives, cutting into Laxmi's soul.

Laxmi, her hands resting on her swollen belly, looked up at Sharad, her eyes pleading with him to understand. "But Sharad, I have done everything to be a good wife. Then why do you go to other women? Don't I love you?"

Sharad snorted, his frustration and anger reaching a boiling point. "It is not about you loving me or not. It is about if I love you. And I don't. I can't even stand your stupid face."

Laxmi hung her head, unable to argue with him. She had always known that Sharad was a womanizer but she hopes once she gets a child, her husband will come back to her. So, she had prayed for a child every night and now, it seemed like her prayers were unanswered and she was pregnant. But it had no effect on the wandering ways of Sharad.

Thinking about Sharad's numerous affairs, Laxmi's heart felt like it was breaking into a million pieces. She fell at Sharad's feet. Sharad pulled her up clutching her hair and pushed her hard. Laxmi's head hit the edge of the rocky surface of the threshold as she fell down. Next, she was in a pool of blood trying to clutch her belly helplessly, as if it promised her unborn child that she would do everything in her power to keep them safe, no matter what.

By the time Ambika reached there, Laxmi had bled to death. Ambika cried as she looked at the dead body of her daughter-in-law lying on the floor.

"What have you done?" she asked Sharad, her voice quivering with fear.

"I didn't mean to kill her," Sharad said. "But she just wouldn't listen to me."

Ambika sighed, tears streaming down her face. "What are we going to do now?"

"We have to make it look like an accident," Sharad said, determination in his voice. "Tell everyone that she fell in the bathroom."

Ambika nodded, fear evident in her eyes. "Okay," she whispered, tears still flowing down her cheeks.

Sharad carried Laxmi's body to the bathroom. He knew he had made a terrible mistake, but he couldn't undo it now. But he had to protect himself at all costs.

30

Ambika's heart was heavy with grief and guilt. She had seen the horrors of violence and had been a silent witness to Sharad's cruel actions. She felt trapped in a world of sadness and fear. But as she heard the cries of the newborn child, her thoughts were interrupted. The tiny cries of the infant, so full of life and innocence, brought a glimmer of hope to Ambika's heart.

She walked towards the crib where the baby was lying, its tiny hands and feet flailing in the air. As she looked at the newborn, she couldn't help but think about the future that lay ahead for it. She wondered if the child would grow up in a world free from the violence and cruelty that surrounded them. The baby boy's mother Mala was sleeping on the nearby bed.

"Oh Lord Jagananth! please protect this child," Ambika prayed as she held the baby close to her chest. "Let it grow up in a world of love and peace."

At that moment, Mala opened her eyes. Maybe they were searching for Sharad. Mala looked at Ambika with a mix of confusion and worry. Ambika knew that Sharad had been distant lately, but she never thought he would be absent during such an important moment. She put her hand on Mala's forehead, gently wiping away the sweat, and said, "Don't worry, my child. I will speak to him. You just focus on taking care of the little one."

Mala tried to smile. Ambika asked, "And what should we call him?"

"Bhagirath," Mala replied.

Ambika smiled at the new mother and the newborn baby. "Bhagirath, a strong name for a strong boy. He will bring you happiness and success, my dear," she said, her voice filled with warmth.

Mala gazed lovingly at her son and whispered, "Yes, he will be my everything. He is my Bhagia."

Ambika took the baby in her arms and gently rocked him

back and forth. "I know Sharad will come around eventually. He will see the love in your son's eyes and realize what he's been missing."

The baby gurgled contentedly as Ambika hummed a lullaby, and Mala watched, feeling a sense of peace wash over her. She was grateful for her mother-in-law's love and support.

"We'll raise Bhagia together," Ambika said, her eyes shining with pride. "He will know the love of a mother and a grandmother."

Mala and Ambika sat there, bonding over the precious new life in their arms, dreaming of a bright future for Bhagia and their family. As Ambika was rocking her grandson gently, she felt a sense of comfort wash over her. Maybe, just maybe, the future was not as bleak as it seemed. Maybe there was hope for a better tomorrow. And at that moment, Ambika felt a small flame of hope flicker within her, a hope that things would get better, a hope that they could find their way back to a life of contentment and togetherness.

31

As the days passed by, Mala felt more and more isolated in her own home. Her husband was now more distant and aloof. He spent all his time with Chandra, flaunting their relationship in front of her. Mala, who was once an innocent girl filled with hope and love, now felt like a forgotten memory in the back of Sharad's mind.

One day, as she sat holding her son Bhagia, she could feel the weight of Sharad's scolding words pressing down on her. He would frequently berate her for no reason, calling her names and belittling and beating her in front of others. Mala, who was once so full of life, now felt like she was slowly being suffocated by Sharad's cruel words.

And to make matters worse, Sharad had no emotional connection with his own son. He showed no love or affection towards Bhagia, leaving his infant son rejected and alone.

Ambika tried to support her and offer her some comfort, but even she was not immune to Sharad's wrath. He would scold her for supporting Mala and giving in to her demands. It was a never-ending cycle of cruelty and abuse.

Despite all of this, Ambika held onto a glimmer of hope. She believed that someday, Sharad would realize what he had done and come back to his son, filled with love and remorse. Maybe even the poor Mala had hoped the same. But as the days passed by and Sharad's cruelty continued, that glimmer of hope slowly faded away, leaving behind only darkness and despair.

32

Mohan stood in front of the mirror, carefully combing his hair and adjusting his clothes. He felt his wife Priti's bitter gaze on him, like a scorching sunburn. "Why are you taking so much time in front of the mirror?" she asked, her voice dripping with sarcasm. "Are you hoping to impress your girlfriend Mala at the shop today?"

She watched as her husband put in extra effort to look presentable and taunted him, "Is your girlfriend Mala visiting the shop today? That's why you're taking so much time in front of the mirror?"

Mohan turned to her, annoyance evident in his voice, "What do you mean by that?"

Priti let out a bitter laugh, "Everyone in the village knew about your love for Mala. But I fell for my father's trap and had to marry you for your newly acquired money and shop. And now I have to bear the consequences."

Mohan's eyes narrowed as he asked, "Do you want to leave then?"

Priti threw her head back and laughed, a cruel sound that echoed in the room. "And let you run to your sweetheart without a care in the world? No thank you, Mohan. I'll stay right here, where I can keep an eye on you."

Mohan knew that there was no reasoning with Priti. But then he was the one to be blamed for this bitter transformation of Priti. He had still carried a torch for his former crush Mala, leaving Priti feeling trapped and unloved in her own marriage. They had not consummated their marriage, adding to her frustration and bitterness. And Mohan could do nothing about it.

So, Mohan grabbed his keys and strode out of the house, determined to put the argument behind him and focus on his work at the shop. But he couldn't shake the feeling that his life was becoming a never-ending cycle of bitterness and resentment. He headed towards the door, leaving Priti behind with her bitter thoughts and unfulfilled desires.

Chapter 7: A New Dusk

33

As Bhagia grew into a 7-month-old, the whole village was openly talking about Sharad and Chandra. They would see him taking Chandra on his bike and romancing with her, going on shopping sprees, and they would report these sightings to Ambika and Mala.

That night, Mala's heart was pounding with fear as she mustered up the courage to confront Sharad. She asked him, her voice shaking, "What's going on between you and Chandra? I've been hearing about your outings with her and the villagers have been talking about it."

Sharad's anger was palpable as he replied, "I want you to leave my house. I want to marry Chandra."

Mala's heart sank at his words. She looked over at Bhagia who was fast asleep and tears filled her eyes. She said, "Where will I go? My poor mother is not in a position to take care of us. I have nowhere to turn."

Falling to her knees, Mala pleaded with Sharad, "You can marry Chandra and bring her home. I'll stay here as a servant. I'll do anything, just please don't leave me and Bhagia on the streets."

Sharad looked at the woman before him, begging at his feet, and he felt a sense of happiness in his heart. Finally, he was going to have his way. "Fine," he said coldly. "But you will do as I say, and you will not cause any problems for me or my new wife."

Mala nodded, tears streaming down her face, as she agreed to Sharad's demands. Maybe she was thinking that her life from now on would be filled with hardships and suffering, but she was willing to bear it all for the sake of her son.

34

As Mohan approached the small house, he could see the tired lines on Ketaki's face. He knew that life had not been easy for her, what with her only daughter and now Ketaki falling regularly sick. He reached the doorstep and knocked on the door.

"Come in, my dear," Ketaki said, as she opened the door for Mohan.

"Aunty, I have brought the money that you asked my mother for," Mohan said, handing over the envelope to Ketaki.

"Thank you, Mohan. I will repay it as soon as I can," Ketaki replied, taking the envelope from Mohan's hand.

"Aunty, don't worry about repaying it. It's just a small help," Mohan assured her.

"But I don't want to burden you and your family," Ketaki said, her voice trembling with emotion.

"Aunty, please don't say that. You and Mala have always been family to us," Mohan replied, placing a comforting hand on her shoulder.

Ketaki smiled and said, "Okay, sit here. I will get a bowl of kheer for you."

Mohan nodded in agreement and waited in the small living room of Mala's house. He took a seat on a creaky wooden chair and looked around the room. It's small, cosy and filled with memories of Mala. Every corner of the room reminded him of her.

Ketaki soon returned with a bowl of hot, sweet kheer. "Here you go, Mohan. I hope you like it," she said with a smile.

Mohan thanked her and took a spoonful of the kheer. It was warm and comforting, just like the memories he associated with Mala. He took another spoon and glanced towards the nearby room.

It was Mala's old room. She used to stay there before her marriage. Mohan could see the bookshelf in the corner of Mala's room. It was filled with various knick-knacks, old worn-out textbooks of Mala and a few photo frames.

"You have it," said Ketaki while going inside the kitchen. "I will pack some for your mother."

Mohan nodded. As Ketaki left, Mohan's gaze fell back again on Mala's bookshelf. He stood up from his seat and walked towards her room, his eyes scanning it. He entered her room and reached near the bookshelf. There was an old framed picture and Mohan couldn't help but take it in his hand. It was Mala, smiling and carefree, just like in the old times. He put it back on the shelf and noticed something tucked away behind the books.

Curious, Mohan reached for the object and brought it out. It was a green bundle of letters, tied neatly with a ribbon.

With a little bit of hesitation, he untied the ribbon and started reading the first letter. As he read one letter after another, his heart filled with shock and disbelief. Suddenly he could hear Ketaki's footsteps and gathered the letters in a hurry and tied the ribbon back around them, placing the bundle back on the shelf.

35

As Sharad and Chandra stood at the door, Mala emerged from the kitchen, her eyes falling upon the two of them. The wedding garlands around their necks were a clear indication of what had happened. Ambika, too, had come out, and both women stood rooted to the ground, staring at the newlyweds with a mixture of shock and disbelief.

"Sharad?" Ambika asked, her voice filled with incredulity. "What have you done?"

"I have married Chandra," Sharad declared, his voice full of pride.

Ambika stepped forward, her face a mask of disbelief. "But Sharad, what about Mala?" she asked. "What will she do now?"

Sharad's face hardened. "Mala can stay on as a servant in the house," he said coldly. "But Chandra is my wife now, and she will be the one to occupy the position of a wife in this house."

Mala's eyes filled with tears as she looked at the man whom she had married and who was the father of her son.

"But how can these two women live under the same roof? Ambika asked as her voice trembled.

"It was Mala who agreed to this," Sharad said with a shrug. "Ask her."

Ambika looked at Mala in disbelief. Mala lowered her eyes. Ambika's heart felt like it was breaking into a million pieces.

"She agreed and you married this home breaker?" asked Ambika looking at Chandra with disgust.

"Yes. Because I love Chandra," Sharad said simply. "And I will do anything to be with her."

Ambika sighed. She had always known that her son Sharad was selfish, but she had never imagined that he would be really bringing a third wife when his second wife is still alive. She looked at Chandra, who stood by Sharad's side, looking pleased with herself.

With that, Sharad and Chandra turned and walked into the house, leaving Mala and Ambika standing at the door, their hearts heavy with sorrow and disappointment.

36

As the morning sun peered through the curtains, Sharad woke up to a brand-new life with his newlywed wife, Chandra, by his side. The sound of birds chirping outside the window created a peaceful background music to their morning. He lazily turned to face Chandra, a content smile playing on his lips, but the smile quickly faded as he remembered the task at hand.

With a sudden burst of energy, he jumped out of bed and bellowed, "Maa, send Mala with tea!" His tone was demanding as if he expected his orders to be followed without fail.

Moments later, the sound of light footsteps could be heard approaching the room. The door creaked open and Mala appeared with a tray of steaming hot tea. As she entered the room, she cast a furtive glance at the newlyweds, her expression a mixture of discomfort and curiosity.

"What are you staring at, Mala? Give us the tea and

leave," Sharad snapped, his tone cold and rude.

Mala flinched at Sharad's words, her expression one of hurt. She approached the bed, her eyes darting between Sharad and his new wife Chandra. Chandra, who was lying next to him, gave a sarcastic smile that sent shivers down Mala's spine. She placed the tray on the bedside table and quietly left the room, her footsteps echoing in the silence.

As Mala closed the door behind her, Sharad took a sip of his tea, his eyes trained on the necklace around Chandra's neck. It's a beautiful gold chain with a crescent moon locket.

"The necklace is beautiful. But I've seen a necklace like this somewhere," he muttered, his tone contemplative.

Chandra shot him a smile, "It's a common kind of necklace. You might have seen it in some other shop."

"Yeah, maybe," Sharad replied absently, his mind lost in thought.

As the morning sun continued to rise, Sharad and Chandra settled back into their bed, the tea forgotten. They talked and laughed, enjoying the start of a new life together.

Chapter 8: The Battle Continues

37

Chandra and Sharad flaunted their love in front of Mala who was left feeling both annoyed and envious. The annoyance and jealousy were evident on her face and in the way she carried herself. As Sharad and Chandra exchanged loving glances and whispered sweet nothings to each other, Mala's eyes darted back and forth between them with a mixture of irritation and resentment. The air was thick with the tension of a broken love triangle, as the two wives stood on opposite ends of the room, each feeling the sting of their own unique heartbreak. Despite the cruel remarks and rude gestures from Chandra and Sharad, Mala stood her ground, silently bearing the weight of their disdain with grace and dignity.

That day as Mala entered the room, she could sense the air was thick with tension. Chandra lay on the bed, her eyes tired and her skin pale. Sharad sat beside her, a concerned look on his face.

"Mala," Sharad called out, "Chandra is feeling a bit under the weather. Could you please bring some mustard oil and give her a foot massage to help with her cold and cough? Go and come back fast you fool!"

Mala nodded and quickly left the room to fetch the

mustard oil. As she returned, she could feel Chandra's gaze upon her, filled with disdain.

Mala stood there, frozen, holding the bottle of mustard oil in her hand. Her mind raced with a million thoughts - why was Sharad treating her so rudely, what did she do to deserve this? She took a deep breath, steeling herself for the task ahead.

Chandra's voice brought her back to reality, sharp and biting, "What are you waiting for? Start massaging my feet!"

Mala complied. She hesitantly knelt down and began to pour the warm oil onto Chandra's feet. Then she started to rub it in. The room was silent except for the sound of the oil being massaged into Chandra's skin. Chandra winced at the touch, "Not so rough, you buffoon! Can't you do anything right?"

Sharad gave an angry look at Mala. Mala couldn't help but feel like she was being used and abused. She felt a knot in her stomach as she wondered what her future with this new family member would be like.

Just then, Sharad got up from his seat and walked towards the door. He paused and turned to face Mala; his tone filled with sarcasm.

"Mala," he chuckled, "If Chandra needs anything, you'll be here to fulfil her every demand."

Mala gritted her teeth, trying to ignore the insults being thrown her way. But it was harder to ignore the sound of Sharad's laughter as he started to leave leaving Mala alone with Chandra. The room was filled with an eerie silence as Mala continued to massage Chandra's feet, her thoughts a mixture of fear and frustration.

38

As Chandra opened the almirah, she saw Mala's saree neatly folded on the shelf. She let out a disdainful huff and turned to Sharad, who was sitting on the bed. "Do something about your servant," Chandra sneered, gesturing towards the saree. "Order her to take her things out of here."

"Mala!" Sharad called out, his voice rough and demanding. "Come here!"

Mala was in the middle of feeding the baby, but she dropped everything and rushed to the room. She stood at the doorway, her eyes downcast and a mix of fear and confusion on her face.

"Take your clothes from the shelf," Sharad said, his tone gruff.

"Chandra doesn't want them cluttering up our space."

Mala hesitantly reached up to the shelf, her hands trembling as she gathered her clothes.

"Ok, I am going to take a bath. By the time I come, I want the shelf empty." Chandra said with a smirk on her face, enjoying the power she held over Mala. Then she left for the bathroom.

But Sharad was impatient with the sluggish Mala. He went ahead and started to throw the clothes off the shelf.

As Sharad threw Mala's clothes from the shelf, a glittering necklace fell from the folds of the fabric, catching Sharad's eye. He picked it up and immediately recognized it as Chandra's necklace, the one he was asking about the previous day; the gold chain with a crescent moon locket. Anger rose within him as he realized that Mala had stolen it from Chandra. He turned to her with a scowl, his eyes blazing with fury.

"What is the meaning of this, Mala?" he bellowed, waving the necklace in front of her. "Did you think you could steal from my wife and get away with it?"

Mala's eyes widened in terror as she saw the necklace in Sharad's hand. She stammered, trying to explain herself, but Sharad was in no mood to listen. He pulled Mala's hair and continues to berate her, his voice growing louder and more strident with every word.

Just then, Chandra came out of the bathroom, curious about the commotion. When she sees the necklace in Sharad's hand, her expression turns to one of shock. "Where did you find that?" she asks, her voice barely above a whisper.

"Mala stole it," Sharad replied, his voice cold and unfeeling. Chandra's eyes widen in disbelief as she turns to face Mala.

"I found it on her saree shelf. Where did you leave it?" asked Sharad.

"I had left it on the table last night," answered Chandra and threw an angry look at Mala.

Mala tried to defend herself, but her words were lost in the face of Chandra's outrage. Sharad joined in, beating, slapping, and kicking Mala for her audacity and calling her names. The two of them continued to hit her, their voices rising in anger and sarcasm until Mala finally fell to the ground and broke down in tears.

39

Mala sat in the dimly lit room, surrounded by memories of her late mother Ketaki. A photo of Ketaki, adorned with a garland, stood prominently in the room. The two women who had been keeping her company, consoling her in her grief, had now left, leaving Mala alone with her thoughts and sorrow.

As she gently rocked her son to sleep, she suddenly heard a noise. She turned around to find Mohan, standing in the doorway of her home, his towering figure casting a shadow across the room. Mohan was a man of few words, but his presence commanded attention. Mala felt a shiver run down her spine as she wondered why he was here unannounced.

Mohan stood in front of Mala; his eyes filled with concern. Mala, on the other hand, was overwhelmed with emotions. She had just lost her mother and suddenly felt all alone in this cruel world.

"What are you doing here, Mohan?" Mala asked, her voice quivering with sadness.

"I couldn't stay away any longer," Mohan replied, taking a step closer to her. "I had to come and see you. Make sure you're okay."

"I'm fine," Mala said, trying to hide her emotions. "Please leave me alone, Mohan. I don't want to be a burden on anyone. It is my fate."

Suddenly Mohan's face changed. He stood in front of Mala with a letter in his hand, waving it tauntingly. "If this is your fate, then what is this?" he asked with confusion on his face.

Mala's heart sank as she saw the letter. "Where did you get this?" she asked, her voice trembling with fear.

"I got not one, but a bunch of letters," Mohan replied with a hint of inquisitiveness in his voice.

Mala quickly got up from her seat and rushed to the bookshelf, frantically searching for the letters. But they were nowhere to be found. She turned back to Mohan with a mixture of confusion and anger. "What have you done with them?" she demanded.

"Oh, don't worry, they're safe with me," Mohan replied nonchalantly.

Mala felt her frustration boiling over. Mala demanded the letter back from Mohan. "Give the letter to me," she said, her voice raising in frustration.

But Mohan stood firm, holding the letter tightly in his hand. "No," he said, with a firm voice.

Mala's anger boiled over. "Then what will you do with this letter? Will you blackmail me and ruin my life?" she accused, her eyes flashing with anger.

Her voice raised in desperation. "All men are the same. They only see opportunity," she added, her voice dripping with sarcasm. But Mohan wasn't going to take her insults lying down. He held the letter up in front of her face, the paper crinkling in his grip. "You are no better than men then," he retorted, his tone matching hers in its sarcasm.

Mala's expression softened as she looked at Mohan. She took a step towards him, her hand reaching out to touch his. "Please don't say that. I will tell you everything," she said, her voice filled with a mixture of desperation and sadness.

Just then, the sound of rain pounding against the roof filled the room as a storm rolled in. Both Mala and Mohan looked towards the door, and there stood Sharad, an umbrella in hand, raindrops dripping from the fabric.

40

The rain beat down upon the earth in a symphony of drops. Chandra lay in bed, listening to the sound of the rain and the occasional clap of thunder. Today she was alone had Sharad had gone to fetch Mala. Suddenly, she heard a knock at her window, jolting her out of her peaceful slumber. She rubbed her eyes and sat up, peering out into the darkness.

A figure stood outside, a hooded cloak hiding their face from view. Chandra's heart beat faster as she cautiously approached the window. She opened it slowly, the sound of the rain getting louder as she did so.

"Who are you?" she asked, her voice trembling even though she knew the answer.

As Chandra slowly opened the door, the sound of raindrops hitting the roof filled the air. The man wrapped in a wet shawl stood before her, shrouded in shadows, his beady eyes glinting in the dim light. Chandra clutched the money tightly in her hand, her heart pounding in her chest.

"This is the last time I'm giving you money," Chandra declared firmly, her voice ringing out over the sound of the rain. The man cackled a creepy sound that made Chandra's skin crawl.

"You say that every time, my dear," the man croaked, his gnarled hand reaching out to snatch the money from Chandra's grasp. "But I always seem to find my way back to you, don't I?"

Chandra gritted her teeth and stepped back, her eyes narrowing.

"Just take the money and go," she hissed.

The man laughed again, a wheezy sound that echoed in the night. "Very well, my dear," he said, tucking the money into the pocket of his ragged coat. "But remember, I always have something on you. Something you don't want the world to know."

With that, the man turned and disappeared into the rain, leaving Chandra standing in the doorway, her heart racing with fear. The rain continued to pour down, washing away the sins of the night and leaving behind a clean slate. But Chandra knew that her past memories would linger, a burden that she would carry with her forever.

Chapter 9: The Mystery

41

The sound of raindrops hitting the pavement echoed through the empty streets as two small girls in crisp, white school uniforms walked hand-in-hand. The girl on the left, Mala, takes in the sights and sounds of the stormy night, lost in memories of her childhood.

Suddenly, a small boy ran up to them, a shy grin spreading across his face as he held out a chocolate. The other girl eagerly took it, but Mala simply watched with a wistful smile. The boy scurried away as the two girls giggled, their laughter ringing through the rain-soaked air.

Mala thought back to a time when life was beautiful, a time when sharing chocolate with a friend was the highlight of the day. As she stood there, the rain streaming down her face, she felt a pang of nostalgia for the days gone by. The sweet memories of her childhood were like a warm blanket, shielding her from the realities of the present.

The sound of the raindrops on the roof was like a lullaby, a comforting symphony of nature that washed away the world's troubles. But the tranquillity was short-lived as Mala remembered what had happened just a few hours before.

Sharad had burst into Mala's house, his presence like a thunderstorm, dark and threatening. He stood there, drenched from the rain, his eyes locked onto Mohan, who stood defiantly but with a hint of apprehension.

"Wow! What a wonderful sight," Sharad sneered, his voice heavy with sarcasm. "Now you must be very happy to romance Mala." His words were like arrows, aimed at Mohan's heart, and they found their target. Mohan's face contorted with anger; his fists clenched at his sides.

"More than thinking about my life," Mohan retorted, his voice rising, "you should think about yourself." But Sharad was in no mood to listen. He stepped forward, his hand raised, ready to strike. But just as he was about to make contact, a voice cried out, "Stop!"

It was Rajni, Mohan's mother, and she stepped between the two men, her eyes blazing with fury. "What is the matter with you two?" she cried. "Fighting like children?" Then she looked at Mohan and said, "Shame on you!"

Sharad's hand dropped to his side, and he stepped back. Mohan too had no answer for Rajni's reprimand, no excuse for his behaviour. With a final glare at Mohan, Sharad turned on his heel and stalked out of the room, the sound of the rain once again filling the silence.

42

The next day, the stormy wind in the sky only added fuel to Sharad's already raging temper as he sat in a chair, with Chandra standing next to him. His anger boiled over as he thought of the scene he had stumbled upon, with Mohan and Mala caught in a romantic moment in the rain. "Only because you sent me there," Sharad seethed, "I had to bring her. Otherwise, I would have never witnessed those two lovebirds cooing in the rain like doves."

Sharad's fists clenched at the thought of Mohan, and he exclaimed, "I would have killed that man on the spot if his mother hadn't arrived just in time." But his anger was not limited to just Mohan. Chandra, too, bore the brunt of his wrath as he yelled, "Now, I can't stand her any longer. Throw her out of my house. She's been sitting like a scourge in my home, anyway."

Chandra, unfazed by Sharad's outburst, calmly replied, "She's after your money, how could she ever leave this house?" But Sharad, his voice rising, countered, "What money? I won't even give her a penny. And I'm not bringing her home." Chandra's eyes narrowed as she retorted, "Then who will do all the household chores? I'm not a maidservant. If she's not there, your mother will ask me to do everything. So, bring her back and make her do all the household chores. Understood?"

Sharad was lost in thought, and after a moment of silence, he muttered, "Yes, you're right. I'll bring her back. But not tomorrow. Let a few more days go." The storm outside mirrored the tumultuous emotions inside Sharad as he grappled with the reality of the situation.

43

The sun had just started to rise as Sharad set out towards the nearby town. Chandra was left alone in the shop, surrounded by the stillness of the morning. As she went about her work, arranging the shelves and tidying up, she couldn't shake off the feeling of being watched. Her senses were on high alert, and she couldn't help but constantly glance over her shoulder.

As she completed her task, the door to the shop slowly creaked open. Chandra spun around, her heart beating in her chest. But there was no one there, just the empty street outside. The only thing that remained was a sense of unease that lingered in the air.

Chandra continued to tidy the shelves but her hands froze mid-reach as she heard the sound of footsteps, slow and deliberate. She cautiously turned around, only to find a silhouette looming in the doorway. The sun was at his back, casting a brilliant halo of light around him and obscuring his face in shadow. The man stood there in silence, not saying a word, and Chandra felt her heart race with a mixture of fear and curiosity.

The only sound in the room was the pitter-patter of raindrops against the windowpanes, creating a haunting melody that seemed to perfectly complement the mysterious figure before her. As the seconds ticked by, Chandra found herself holding her breath, waiting for the man to speak or make a move. But he remained still and silent as if he were a statue carved from stone.

The moment was tense and eerie, with an air of mystery that left Chandra on edge. She couldn't help but wonder who this stranger in the shadow was and why he had come to the shop. And as the rain continued to pour outside, she felt as though she were standing on the threshold of a dark and unknown world.

44

As the sun rose on the horizon, Ambika was in the kitchen preparing breakfast for the family. Chandra, whom Ambika had nicknamed a 'couch potato', was lying on the couch in the living room, unwilling to help. Ambika was tired from all the household chores and was struggling to make breakfast on her own. Suddenly, she remembered the time when Mala was still living in their house and helping her with the chores.

"Why did this witch come to my house?" Ambika said to herself,

"Mala was a such blessing. She was such a big help in the house. How will I do all the work?"

Chandra who was lazily lying on the couch overheard Ambika's words and decided to take advantage of the situation. She lazily got up and said, "Oh, so now you need a maid to do all your work. Well, I'm not one. You'll have to manage on your own."

Ambika, who was fed up with Chandra's attitude, raised her voice and said, "Why should I manage on my own when you are here? Why don't you help me for once instead of lying around all day?"

This argument between Ambika and Chandra caught the attention of Sharad who was passing by the living room. He had heard enough of their bickering and decided to put an end to it.

"Enough," Sharad said, "I'm going to bring Mala back to our home. Now both of you please shut up." And with that, Sharad got on his bike and set off to his shop. He was determined to bring Mala back from her village the next day. He knew that his mother was in dire need of help and he couldn't let her suffer anymore. He would bring Mala back and restore peace in the house.

45

The morning sun was just starting to rise, casting a soft orange glow on the deserted streets. Mohan stepped out of his house. As Mohan left his house, his steps were slow and deliberate. His eyes darted around, scanning the empty streets for any signs of prying eyes. He knew that what he was about to do was dangerous, and he was determined to keep it a secret. The rain from the previous night had left the ground slick and slippery, but Mohan didn't let it slow him down. He pressed on; each step was taken with care as he approached his workshop.

Mohan cautiously approached the entrance of his workshop. He quickly fumbled with the key, unlocking the door and slipping inside. The room was dimly lit, but Mohan made his way towards a wooden shelf in the corner. He reached for a small, rectangular box, his hands shaking as he did so. He looked around one last time, before slipping the box into his pocket and quickly making his way back to the door.

He glanced over his shoulder, peering into the shadows to make sure that no one was watching. The sound of his footsteps echoed through the quiet streets as he made his way back home, his mind racing with thoughts of what the future might hold.

Despite his best efforts, Mohan couldn't shake the feeling of unease that had settled over him. He was filled with a sense of foreboding as if the thing in his pocket was a ticking time bomb that could detonate at any moment. With each step he took, the suspense grew more intense, until it seemed like the weight of the world was bearing down on him. But still, he pressed on, determined to keep his secrets safe.

Chapter 10: The Mystery Deepens

46

As the sun began to rise, Mohan woke up from his slumber, his mind racing with thoughts. He got out of bed, trying to be as quiet as possible, but his wife Priti still managed to stir from her sleep, her eyes following Mohan as he made his way out of the room. She watched him as he walked out the door, a sense of suspicion creeping up on her.

Mohan made his way to a serene field, surrounded by tall, green grass that swayed gently in the wind, his heart pounding in his chest. And there, waiting for him, was a figure shrouded in a shawl. It was Mala. Her eyes lit up as she saw him approach.

"Are you leaving?" Mohan asked her, his voice soft.

"Yes," Mala replied, her voice filled with sadness. "Sharad will be coming home today. I asked you to meet me here, in this field."

Mohan pulled a green packet from his pocket and handed it to her. "Here," he said.

Mala's eyes sparkled as she took the bundle of letters from him. She smiled, thanking him. "Thank you, Mohan," she said. "You have always been there for me."

With a last look at Mohan, Mala turned and disappeared into the fields, the green packet of letters held tightly in her hand. Mohan watched her go, a sense of mystery surrounding her as she disappeared into the morning mist.

47

Mohan headed for his home. As Mohan entered the house, Priti was waiting for him on the veranda, with a curious expression on her face. She was taken aback when Mohan swept her up in his arms and carried her to the bedroom. Priti couldn't believe the sudden change in Mohan's behaviour towards her, but despite her surprise, she felt a flutter of happiness in her heart.

Mohan laid her down on the bed and looked into her eyes, filled with love and affection. He tenderly brushed back her hair, caressing her cheek with the back of his hand. Priti felt herself melting under his touch, giving in to the love that she had always known was there.

As she lay down on the bed, her eyes closed, surrendering herself to Mohan's gentle touch. He ran his fingers through her hair, caressing her skin, and planting gentle kisses on her neck.

As they lay in each other's arms, the outside world faded away, leaving only the two of them in a cocoon of love and warmth. They whispered sweet nothings to each other and gazed into each other's eyes, lost in the moment. The two of them made love, each moment a celebration of their deep and abiding love for each other. As they lay entwined in each other's arms, Priti sighed contentedly, snuggling closer to Mohan. He held her tight, closing his eyes as he savoured this moment of pure happiness.

As the sun shone brightly, casting a warm golden light over the room, Mohan and Priti lay together, basking in the afterglow of their love. And at that moment, nothing else mattered but the love they shared, a love as timeless and eternal as the stars in the sky. The sun gradually rose higher in the sky, but they paid it no heed, content in their love for each other. It was as if they had rediscovered their love, just like a blooming flower in the springtime.

48

It was noon when Sharad and Mala embark on a journey back to Sharad's home. The sun beats down mercilessly on the road ahead, but they forge ahead, with Sharad at the handlebars and Mala seated behind him, cradling Bhagia in her lap.

As they journeyed on, they suddenly came upon a disturbing sight - a drunkard lay dying on the side of the road, the victim of a terrible accident. Sharad and Mala slowed their bike and approached the body cautiously, with heavy hearts. Mala took a quick look at the body and then turned away, clearly disturbed by the sight. The air was filled with sadness and despair.

Despite the sadness that lingered in the air, they continued their journey. Soon, they arrived at Sharad's home. Ambika had gone to the temple. Chandra, Sharad's wife, greeted them at the door, her eyes scanning Mala from head to toe.

Chandra handed her a pile of clothes, and Mala understood her duty. She was there to do the household chores, to serve and cater to the whims of Maya and Sharad.

"Here you go, Mala," Chandra said, thrusting the clothes into her hands. "Get these washed as soon as you can. I need them back in my almirah by tonight."

Mala took the clothes silently, understanding the

command in Chandra's voice. She knew that she was expected to do all the household chores, and she didn't mind it one bit. She was just happy to be back in the familiar surroundings of Sharad's house where she had her mother-in-law who loved her like a daughter. She felt a sense of comfort wash over her as she began her chores.

49

As the stars twinkled in the sky and the moon cast a warm glow over the home, Sharad sat down to have his meal. The delicious aroma of spices and herbs filled the air, a testament to Mala's culinary skills. But Sharad had nothing to do with it.

After finishing his food, Sharad made his way to Chandra's room where she was brushing her hair, her silhouette cast against the candlelight. He approached her with a smile, taking her hand and leading her to the bed.

As they lay down, Sharad pulled her close, kissing her neck tenderly. Chandra's heart raced with anticipation as he held her close, the warmth of his embrace enveloping her completely. The world seemed to fade away as they lost themselves in the moment, their love as strong and as true as ever.

However, as the night wore on, Sharad began to feel restless. Despite the romantic atmosphere, he felt a sense of unease and discomfort, a strange feeling creeping over him. Chandra noticed and asked what was wrong, but Sharad could only shake his head and hold his chest, a sharp pain suddenly gripping him. Chandra screamed in terror as Sharad fell back onto the bed, his eyes closed and his breathing shallow.

The sound of Chandra's scream echoed through the night, rousing Ambika and Mala from their slumber. They rushed to the bedside, their hearts heavy with fear and uncertainty. What had happened to Sharad? Would he be, okay? These questions and more swirled through their minds as they stood there, watching over him, their hearts full of love and concern.

Chapter 11: The Aftermath

50

Days passed after Sharad's sudden and tragic passing, and tensions between Chandra and Mala only continued to rise. Chandra, still grieving the loss of her husband, began to direct her anger and frustration towards the unsuspecting Mala. Every little thing, from the food she cooked to the way she cleaned, was met with harsh criticism from Chandra.

Mala, equally wounded by Sharad's death, was quick to fire back. The two women bickered and fought like two hens over scraps, each blaming the other for Sharad's death.

Ambika, being the matriarch of the household, was fed up with their constant bickering. She scolded them both, her voice echoing through the halls like a thunderclap. "You two are acting like children," she chided. "How can you blame each other for Sharad's death? It was fate, a cruel twist of fate that took him from us."

But the two women paid little heed to Ambika's words, and their bickering continued day in and day out. They were locked in an endless cycle of blame, each determined to place the fault for Sharad's passing on the other.

Despite her efforts to bring peace to the household, Ambika found herself siding with Mala more often than not. "At least she's trying," she thought to herself, as she watched

Chandra snap at Mala for forgetting to refill the tea kettle.

Though the house was not harmonious for a long time, now the home was filled with more tension and discontent, a far cry from the warm and loving atmosphere Ambika would have hoped.

51

It was a typical day in the house of Sharad, or so it seemed. Tensions were running high between Chandra and Mala, two women who were once united by their love for the same man. But as the days passed, their relationship soured, and they found themselves bickering over small things, like a pile of wet clothes left in the courtyard.

It all started when Chandra came out to the veranda, looking for her dry clothes, but instead, she found them drenched once again. Frustrated, she turned to Mala and accused her of not bringing the clothes inside. Mala, in turn, became defensive and the two women began to argue, their voices growing louder with each passing moment.

Soon enough, the rest of the village was drawn to the commotion. They gathered around the house, watching as the two women pulled each other's hair, their screams echoing through the air. Ambika, had enough of the bickering and decided to take action.

She marched over to the door of the room where Mala and Chandra were locked and called out, "That's enough!" With a flick of her wrist, she locked the door behind her, trapping the two women inside. "You two won't come out until you've learned to get along," she declared.

As the hours passed, the two women continued to bicker, their voices growing hoarse from all the shouting and

Ambika could hear it. But eventually, they ran out of things to say, and there was nothing left but silence.

Chandra and Mala slowly simmered down, until they found themselves sitting on the floor of the room in silence. Their eyes met, and for the first time in what felt like ages, there was a glimmer of understanding in their gaze. Chandra stood up, slowly walking over to where Mala was seated. She reached out and gently brushed her hand through Mala's hair, the touch sending shivers down her spine. Chandra leaned in, her lips softly brushing against Mala's cheek before finally, their lips met in a tender, loving kiss. It was a kiss filled with the longing that had built up between them, the promise of a new beginning. When they parted, Mala's eyes were alight with a coy smile, and Chandra too couldn't help but smile. "It took time," she whispered, "but it was worth it."

Chapter 12: The Past Catches Up

52

The scene was chaotic, as the villagers gathered in a frenzy, shouting and jeering at the two women lying on the ground. Little Mala pressed herself against the wall, trying to stay hidden, trying to make sense of what was happening. She heard snippets of conversation, snippets of hate and bigotry that made her heartache.

"How could they do this?" one man was saying, his voice filled with disgust. "They're an abomination, a disgrace to our village."

"They deserve to be punished," another man chimed in, his eyes cold and hard. "They bring shame to us all."

A woman, her hair pulled back in a tight bun, nodded in agreement. "Lesbians, that's what they are," she sneered. "Disgusting creatures. They should be locked up and left to rot."

Little Mala felt a lump form in her throat. She had never heard of such a thing before, never heard of people being hated and punished simply for loving someone of the same gender. And yet, here it was, happening right before her very eyes.

As the two women were dragged away, Mala's heart went out to them. She felt a strange connection to them as if they were somehow linked by a shared experience, a shared pain. And as she peeked through the peephole into the room where they were being held, she felt a deep sadness and a longing to help.

But as she was about to turn away, a hand patted her shoulder, causing her to jump in fear. She spun around, only to see a villager. She quickly gathered her wits and fled the scene, her heart pounding in her chest.

53

The 80s,

It was a day like any other in the small village, except for the rain. The skies had opened up and a downpour had transformed the once-parched earth into a sea of mud. But for young Mala and Chandra, it was a day to be remembered. They were the best of friends, having grown up together in the village, and this was their time to revel in the joys of childhood.

Young Mohan, who had always had a crush on Mala, had come to school with a special treat for her. He approached her, a shy smile on his face, and offered her chocolate. Mala's eyes lit up in delight, and she took the chocolate, eager to taste its sweetness.

As they laughed and played in the rain, the two girls were oblivious to the world around them. They were lost in the joys of childhood, with no worries or cares. And as they ran and splashed in the puddles, they were the very picture of happiness.

But little did they know that this would be the last day of their carefree existence. Soon, they would be thrust into a world of conflict and hatred, where the forces of intolerance would threaten to tear them apart. And as they grew up, they would come to realize that their love for each other was a crime in the eyes of the villagers.

Yet through it all, they would stand by each other, even as the world around them threatened to crumble. For in each other, they had found a love that was pure and true, a love that would endure the test of time. And so, even as the rain stopped and the sun shone down on the small village once again, the two girls held hands and whispered to each other, promising to always be best friends.

54

The 90s

As they grew up, young Mala and Chandra started to realize that they had more than just a friendship between them. They felt an undeniable physical attraction to each other, an attraction that they could not ignore. They started to sneak away from their respective homes and meet at a secluded spot in the forest. The spot was hidden by the tall trees and was surrounded by the melodious sounds of chirping birds and rustling leaves.

They would spend hours sitting by the side of a bubbling brook, their hearts pounding with excitement as they talked about their feelings for each other.

They had finally found the one person who understood them in a way that no one else ever could. They laughed, shared their hopes and dreams, and explored the depth of their feelings for each other.

The forest became their secret haven, a place where they could be themselves without fear of judgment or persecution. They knew that their relationship was unconventional, but they didn't care. They were in love, and nothing else mattered.

As the sun started to set and the sky turned a brilliant shade of orange and red, they would reluctantly make their way back to their homes. They would part with a kiss and the promise to meet again soon. It was a sweet and tender moment, one that they would never forget.

Despite the risks, they knew that they couldn't stay away from each other for long. They were two halves of a whole, and they were meant to be together.

55

But all too soon, Mala and Chandra's world was torn apart. Mala's father passed away, leaving her to pick up the pieces of her shattered life. She had to leave school and help her mother to take care of the family's farm, putting her future on hold. Meanwhile, Chandra was sent to the city to live with her uncle and aunt, who had taken her in after she lost her parents.

As they said their goodbyes at their special place, both girls were consumed by grief. Tears streamed down their cheeks as they clung to each other, unwilling to let go. They knew that this might be the last time they would ever see each other. Chandra pulled away first, giving Mala a note. "I will be back one day," she whispered, her voice breaking with emotion.

With a heavy heart, Mala watched as Chandra walked away until she was nothing but a distant memory. The thought of losing her love was too much to bear, and Mala felt a sharp pang in her chest as if her heart was being torn in two. She held the note tightly, as if it was a precious treasure, knowing that it was all she had left of Chandra.

The next few days were a blur for Mala, as she tried to come to terms with her loss. Every time she closed her eyes, she saw Chandra's face and heard her voice. She knew that the road ahead would be difficult, but she was determined to keep her promise to her beloved. One day, she would find her way back to Chandra, no matter what it took.

56

As the years passed, Chandra's longing for her childhood love, Mala, only grew stronger. Finally, at the age of twenty-three, she returned to her small village, her heart overflowing with the hope of being reunited with the one she loved. But her joy was short-lived, as she was quickly reminded of the harsh realities she had been trying to escape.

"I'm back, my love," Chandra whispered, as she approached the secluded spot where she and Mala used to play as children.

Mala's eyes lit up with joy at the sight of her long-lost love, and she threw herself into Chandra's waiting arms. They held each other tightly, tears streaming down their faces as they shared a kiss that was filled with the passion and longing of years apart.

"I missed you so much," Mala whispered between sobs.

Chandra stroked her hair and looked into her eyes, her heart breaking at the pain she saw there. "I know, my love. I'm so sorry for everything. I had to leave for the city. Once I started working, I had to escape my uncle, who was always after me for money. And now my aunt has passed away, and I'm once again on the run."

Mala's eyes filled with tears as she listened to Chandra's tale of hardship and pain. "I don't care about any of that," she said, determination in her voice. "All I care about is being with you."

"And I feel the same, my love," Chandra replied, kissing her tenderly. "Together, we can overcome anything."

As they clung to each other, both women knew that the journey ahead would be filled with challenges, but they were determined to face them together, as long as they had each other's love to sustain them.

"Wait, I have a gift for you," said Chanda. Mala was intrigued. Chandra reached out and placed the delicate gold chain in Mala's hand. "This necklace is a symbol of us, our love, our friendship," she said, her voice filled with emotion. "I want you to have it, to remember me by. This is the moon. It's me, Chandra and this is the chain, it's you, Mala. We will always be together. See, I am wearing one too." Chandra uncovers her neck and shows her chain to Mala.

Mala held the pendant between her fingers, gazing at the shimmering crescent moon. "It's beautiful," she whispered, a single tear sliding down her cheek. "I can't bear the thought of being apart from you."

Chandra wrapped her arms around Mala, pulling her close. "I know, my love," she said, kissing the top of Mala's head. "But we'll find a way. We have to."

Mala leaned into Chandra's embrace, closing her eyes. She couldn't forget the image of two women, just like her and Chandra, beaten to death in her village square. The memories of their screams and the angry mob still haunted her dreams.

"We have to be careful," she said, her voice trembling. "The world isn't always kind to people like us."

Chandra nodded; her expression serious. "I know," she

said. "But we can't give up on each other. We'll find a way to be together, no matter what."

She took the necklace from Mala and fastened it around her neck, then pulled her into a warm embrace. "We're Chandramala, forever and always."

57

"Do you know the story of the mothers of King Bhagirath, the king who had brought the sacred Ganga River to this planet earth?" that day asked Chandra when they spending a lazy afternoon in the forest.

"No, I don't," replied Mala. "Tell me, please," Mala requested as her eyes sparkled with wonder.

Chandra, seeing the eagerness in Mala's gaze, smiled warmly and began to weave the tale. Mala put her head on Chandra's lap. Chandra started, "In ancient times, the Surya Vansh Dynasty of the Ramayana was ruled by King Dilipa. Despite his power and influence, he was troubled by one thing - he had no son or heir to carry on his legacy. The fact that Lord Ram was said to descend from the same bloodline added to his worries. He was determined to find a solution to this problem."

The Queen continued, "King Dilipa sought the help of the family priest, who promised the frightened wives that a son would be born soon. He urged the ladies to engage in an unusual connection, which was an unprecedented act for widows who were traditionally supposed to live a solitary and celibate life."

"But Chandra and Mala, the two widowed queens, were not bound by convention. They defied tradition and embarked on a journey of love and desire. With the blessing of Kamadeva, the god of love and desire, they indulged in a passionate love affair, making love and kissing deeply during the monsoon season, which was considered a time of romance."

"Their connection was not just a sexual act to preserve the kingdom, but the beginning of a true love story between two co-wives. It was a celebration of their rebellious spirit, an insatiable yearning that rendered them powerless in the face of it," Chandra concluded, a smile playing on her lips.

Mala listened intently to the tale, marvelling at the bravery and determination of these two women. She felt a deep connection to their story, and it filled her with pride and inspiration. As she drifted off to a smile, she couldn't help but wonder what adventures lay ahead for her and Chandra, her only true love.

58

Now, every day, Mala and Chandra would secretly meet each other, their hearts overflowing with love and affection for one another. They would find a quiet and secluded place where they could bask in the warmth of their love, far from the judgmental eyes of the world. As they sat together, hand in hand, they would talk about their hopes, dreams, and fears, cherishing every moment spent in each other's company.

The world may have been harsh and unforgiving to them, but in each other's arms, they found solace and a sense of belonging. They felt alive in a way that they never had before, and they knew that their love was the only thing that truly mattered. They were two halves of a whole, and their love was the unbreakable bond that kept them together.

Every day, as they parted ways, they would promise to meet again, and the anticipation of their next rendezvous would keep them going, fueling their passion and love for each other. Despite the danger and the fear of being caught, they continued to meet each other in secret, every day, their love growing stronger with each passing moment.

One day, as Mala and Chandra sat under the shady trees near their secret meeting place, Mala confided in her beloved friend with a heavy heart. "Chandra, I've received two marriage proposals."

"Really?" Chandra asked, surprised. "Who are they from?"

"One is from Mohan," Mala replied, her voice tinged with sadness. "And the other is from Sharad."

Chandra couldn't help but laugh at the mention of Mohan. "Poor Mohan, still pining for you after all these years."

But then her laughter faded, and she grew serious. "We need to find out more about Sharad. I'll do some research. We can't take any chances."

"But why can't we just run from home? We can be together," asked Mala.

Chandra gave a helpless smile. "Where would we go? We will be killed by our own villagers if we get caught. And if we run away, how will we be together? How will we stay under the same roof? What would be our relationship? Will society accept us?"

"Then?" mala enquired innocently.

"We have to find out a solution. I will find a way. We will go by the rules set by society and then we will break them in our way," said Chandra confidently.

Mala nodded, grateful for Chandra's support and love. "I trust you, Chandra. You always know what's best for us."

Chandra took Mala's hand in hers and looked into her eyes. "I'll always protect you and make sure you're happy, Mala. That's all I ever want."

And with that, the two women sat hand in hand, basking in the warmth of their love and the comfort of each other's presence.

Chapter 13: The Conspiracy

59

Chandra, disguised in a dupatta, trailed Sharad's every move, her eyes keen and watchful. As she observed him at a local fair, she was repulsed by the sight that met her eyes. Sharad had no qualms about touching women inappropriately, his lecherous gaze roaming over the bodies of the fairer sex. Chandra watched in horror as he brazenly molested women, taking advantage of their vulnerability. Her heart sank as she watched him disappear into a brothel, his intentions unmistakably foul.

Chandra couldn't believe what she was seeing. The man who had been considered a suitable match for Mala was nothing but a monster in disguise. Chandra made a mental note of every detail she saw, determined to confide everything with Mala.

As she made her way back to meet Mala, Chandra was filled with a sense of urgency. "Mala," she said, her voice filled with the weight of her findings. "I've followed Sharad, and what I've seen is deplorable. He touches women inappropriately, looks at them with lust in his eyes, molests them and visits prostitutes."

Mala was shocked and asked for more details. Chandra recounted the evidence, painting a vivid picture of Sharad's misdeeds. "He is not a man to be trusted," she concluded. "But then he is the perfect man we need."

And so, Chandra and Mala hatched a scheme. Mala would accept Sharad's proposal, and they would use this opportunity to bring Chandra into his life.

60

Meanwhile Mala and Chandra were writing letters to each other filled with the essence of their love, like drops of honey on a page, each word drizzled with the sweetness of their emotions. The ink bled with the passion of their hearts, each letter a window into the soul of their love. They wrote of the sunsets they shared, the laughter they shared, and the dreams they nurtured together. And as they wrote, they knew that each letter was a bond that connected them, a lifeline to the other's heart, an eternal reminder of the love they held for each other. The letters were like the fluttering of butterfly wings, gentle, yet with the power to move mountains, for their love was as wild and free as the winds that carried the letters to their waiting hearts.

After Mala's wedding, she had to leave her bundle of letters behind as she was scared of being caught by her new husband. Her mother's place was comparatively a safer haven.

As Chandra had made up her mind, she started her mission to manipulate Sharad. She slowly started to make her presence known in his life, working as his shop attendant.

When Mala had seen Chandra in Sharad's shop for the first time, her heart skipped a bit. The two women locked eyes, sharing a mysterious smile that only they could understand. Sharad was completely oblivious to this exchange, as he was too caught up in his own thoughts. But for Mala and Chandra, this was a moment of triumph. They had been working towards this plan for so long, and now, their hard work was finally paying off. As they walked away, their smiles still lingering on their faces, they knew that this was just the beginning of a much bigger game they were playing.

Before Sharad knew it, he was falling in love with Chandra. Chandra was a master of manipulation and knew exactly how to make a man fall for her. She knew how to play with his emotions, making him feel wanted and loved. With her sweet smile and charming personality, she had won Sharad's heart completely.

As Sharad's love for her grew stronger, so did his trust in her. Chandra used this to her advantage, slowly but surely revealing her true intentions to him. Her plan was working perfectly and soon enough, she had Sharad exactly where she wanted him.

The once lustful and abusive man had now become a love-sick puppy, ready to do anything for the woman he loved. Chandra had succeeded in her mission, and Sharad was now under her control.

Every day, she would make sure to give a special touch to his food by adding just the right amount of a special masala. It wasn't long before Sharad started to take notice of her culinary skills and her efforts to make his food taste better. But little did he know that in the guise of masala, Chandra was feeding him a slow poison.

61

Mala also had to hide her chain from Sharad. When Sharad was searching for his missing watch, maybe he had stumbled upon Mala's chain and took notice of it. Nevertheless, later when he saw the exact same chain around Chandra's neck, luckily, he could not remember where he had seen it before. So, both Mala and Chandra had breathed a sigh of relief, having successfully kept their secret hidden from Sharad.

On the day when Sharad had asked Mala to massage Chandra's feet after Sharad left the room, the two women hugged each other, both deeply feeling the weight of the secret they had to keep. They knew that their love was forbidden and that they had to be careful, but they couldn't help but cry out their pain to each other.

Mala was looking at the bites and scratches Sharad had given her. Chandra had to tolerate the aggressive lovemaking of Sharad only by clenching her teeth and fists. Tears filled her eyes as she realized the pain that Chandra had gone through for their love. As she touched Chandra's bruises, the two women cried, embracing each other tightly. They knew that their love for each other had led them down this painful path, but it was a sacrifice they were willing to make.

Chandra looked into Mala's eyes and saw the pain of the domestic abuse she was going through every day. Mala, on the other hand, could see the same pain reflected in Chandra's eyes. They both knew that they were suffering, but they also knew that their love was strong enough to get them through.

As they pulled away, the two women smiled mysteriously at each other, a hint of their secret love shining through. They both knew that their love was not just about them, but about the strength and courage it took to stand up for what they believed in, even in the face of adversity.

Their love was a mystery, hidden from the world, but it was a mystery that they cherished deeply, for it was the only thing that gave their lives meaning. They were two women in love, willing to go to great lengths to protect and preserve their love, no matter what the world may think.

62

As one day Sharad accused Mala of stealing the chain, and Chandra had listened to it in from the bathroom. She took off her own identical chain, determined to protect her beloved Mala. With a steady hand, she stepped out of the bathroom, holding the chain in her palm.

She had asked the reason for the commotion, feigning ignorance. Then Sharad turned to Mala, his eyes blazing with anger and accused her of stealing Chandra's chain. That day just to show Sharad, Chandra had to hit Mala, but her heart was crying.

Thus, Chandra and Mala's love for each other continued to grow stronger even while they were living in the same house with Sharad. They would often sneak away to be alone together, their secret rendezvous filled with passion and affection. But in front of others, they would put on a facade of animosity, constantly bickering and fighting to keep their secret relationship hidden. They were experts in deception, and their acting skills were unparalleled. They would argue loudly and publicly, all the while exchanging secret smiles and meaningful glances when no one was looking.

They were living a double life, playing a dangerous game of hide and seek with their true feelings for each other. Despite the risks, they were both willing to do whatever it took to protect their love and keep it hidden from the world.

63

Mala and Chandra's secret meetings became more frequent and intense as they discussed the horrors of living with Sharad. One day, as they sat hidden away from prying eyes, Mala opened up to Chandra about the true nature of Sharad.

"Chandra," whispered Mala, her voice trembling with fear, "Sharad has killed his first wife Laxmi. He's a monster, a real monster."

Chandra listened intently, her heart racing with fear and anger. She knew that she had to protect both of them from the monster they were living with.

"I know," replied Chandra, "I've been trying to gather evidence to expose him, but it's not easy. But I will find a way."

Chandra's words gave Mala hope, and she felt a glimmer of light in the dark days she was living through. The two women hugged each other tightly, and for a moment, their fears and worries melted away.

But their troubles were far from over. Chandra also revealed to Mala that her uncle had become a constant nuisance, regularly asking for money. She was struggling to get rid of him and keep him at bay, but she was determined to do what it took to protect themselves.

The two women hugged each other again, both feeling the weight of their troubles, but determined to see it through to the end. They knew that their secret romance was not just for their own happiness, but for their survival as well. They promised each other that they would never give up, no matter what came their way.

When they were parting, Mala's eyes filled with tears. "Put an end to this soon. I can't take it anymore," she said, "We need to get out of here."

Chandra put a comforting arm around her beloved. "Don't worry, I have a plan. I know someone who can help us." And the man was none other than Mohan.

64

Mohan had chosen a day when Sharad was not in the shop. He had gone into the shop, watching as Chandra cleaned the shelves and dusted the counter. He was Chandra's childhood friend too but he was never in touch with her once she left the village. After reading the letter hidden in the green packet, everything finally made sense to him.

He took a deep breath and pushed open the door, making his way to where Chandra stood. She looked up, her eyes meeting his.

"Why are you two doing this?" Mohan asked, his voice low. "I realized your true relationship after reading the letter."

Chandra's expression softened as she looked at Mohan. "You love Mala, don't you?" she asked, her voice barely above a whisper.

Mohan nodded, unable to form the words to express the depth of his feelings.

"We are doing this only for love," Chandra continued. "If you expose us, either we will be killed by Sharad like his first wife. But then what will you get?"

Mohan sighed, knowing she was right. He couldn't bear the thought of something happening to either of them.

"I understand," he said, his voice barely above a whisper. "I just want to make sure you both are safe."

Chandra gave him a sad smile, her eyes shining with unshed tears. "We are doing what we have to do," she said. "For love." "And we want your help."

Mohan looked at Chandra with confusion, "What can I do?"

Chandra replied, "I know you have access to cyanide in your jewellery workshop. We need it to put an end to

Sharad's monstrous behaviour once and for all. That cyanide will induce heartache and no one will suspect us."

Mohan was taken aback, "Are you suggesting we kill him? That's a dangerous game, Chandra. We can't just go around killing people. And anyway, it's a crime. Not only a crime but a sin."

Chandra pleaded, "Think about Laxmi, his first wife who was killed by him. He deserves to pay for his crimes, and we are just ensuring that justice is served. This is not a sin; it is our duty."

"It was always your plan, wasn't it? To choose Sharad for Mala, to get into Sharad's life and ultimately to kill him," asked Mohan with a curious voice.

"This was our only way," said Chandra with a firm voice. Then she started pleading again. "Please help us, Mohan. We need to act fast. Please do it for Mala's happiness."

Mohan was in a dilemma, but he couldn't deny the urgency in Chandra's voice. He finally agreed, "Okay, I'll help you. But we need to be very careful with the cyanide. One wrong move and it could be the end for all of us."

Chandra breathed a sigh of relief, "Thank you, Mohan. We will be forever grateful to you. We will make sure to use it with care."

As Mohan left the shop, Chandra felt relieved. She knew that it wasn't a sin to kill a monster like Sharad. She had no feelings or guilt. Instead, she was determined to protect her beloved and make sure that justice was served.

65

Mohan woke up early the next day, his mind heavy with the weight of his recent conversation with Chandra. He had made a decision, one that went against his morality, but for the sake of love, he was willing to take the risk. He went to his workshop, his heart racing as he gathered the cyanide that he had promised to give to Mala. He carefully placed the small vial of poison into a green letter packet, just as he had promised Chandra. The packet was small, but it held within it a power that could change their lives forever.

As he walked toward the field, his mind was filled with a mixture of fear and determination. He knew the dangers of what he was doing, but he was willing to face them for the sake of love. He arrived at the field and saw Mala waiting for him. He handed her the packet, and she took it from him with a smile. He could see the gratitude and love in her eyes, and it filled him with a sense of pride.

Mohan watched as Mala walked away, the green packet clutched tightly in her hand. He felt a mix of emotions as he thought of the consequences of his actions. But he knew that he had made the right decision, for love was worth the risk. And with that thought, he turned and walked away, hoping that he had made the right choice.

After coming to know the truth about Mala and Chandra's relationship, Mohan was filled with sympathy and admiration for their love. He realized how far they were willing to go for each other, even if it meant sacrificing their own happiness. Despite the difficulties they faced, they still loved each other deeply. This realization made Mohan see his own relationship with Priti in a new light, and he was filled with gratitude for her love and support. He realized that he too should cherish his relationship with Priti, and he consummated his marriage with her, committing himself fully to their love. It was a reminder to the world that love knows no boundaries and that true love will always find a way.

66

When Mala had come back from home, she was filled with emotions as she recounted eyes on her beloved Chandra. Later, they met secretly in the backyard. Mala took a deep breath and related the accident she had witnessed earlier on the road. Chandra listened intently, as Mala spoke about how she saw a drunkard lying dead on the spot."

Chandra felt a sudden jolt as she heard this, her heart racing as she asked, "Who was he?"

"It was your uncle," replied Mala.

He had been constantly taking money from Chandra and threatening to reveal her true identity to Sharad. Despite his disgusting behaviour, Chandra had been bearing with him for a long time. She felt a sense of relief wash over her, as she realized that her uncle, who had been causing her so much trouble, was now gone. She knew that the way her uncle was addicted to alcohol, one day he would meet with such a terrible fate.

Chandra closed her eyes and whispered, "It's a sign from God that all things will fall into place."

Mala hugged her tightly and whispered, "I'll always be here for you, Chandra. No matter what happens."

"You remember what you have to do tonight, don't you?" asked Chandra.

Mala smiled and nodded. The two women stood there, lost in their embrace, as the sun began to set and the world around them went quiet. They knew that their love for each other was strong enough to overcome any obstacle that lay ahead.

67

That night, as Mala made her way to the kitchen, she took a deep breath, steeling herself for what was to come. She knew what needed to be done and she was determined to see it through. Chandra stood to watch by the door; her eyes filled with determination as she waited for Mala to carry out their plan.

Mala mixed the overdose of cyanide into the food, making sure to mix it thoroughly so that it would be undetectable. She then made her way back to the dining room, where Sharad was eagerly awaiting his meal. As she placed the plate in front of him, she couldn't help but feel a twinge of guilt in her heart. But she reminded herself that this was all for love and for justice meant for all the wrongs that Sharad had committed.

That night while making love, Chandra was watching closely, waiting for the poison to take effect. It wasn't long before Sharad started to feel the effects, his face contorting in pain as he clutched at his chest. Chandra called for Mala and Ambika. Chandra watched in urgency as Sharad fell to the ground, his body writhing in agony as he took his last breaths. By the time Mala and Ambika reached, everything was over.

At that moment, Chandra and Mala were filled with a sense of relief, knowing that their love has won and justice had finally been served for all the lives that Sharad had ruined. Their heart celebrated the fact that they had finally achieved the goal that they so desperately sought. Their plan was successful. Now they both were together, under one roof and nothing could separate them.

Mala and Chandra were still kissing in the room locked by their mother-in-law Ambika, whom they both shared. It was a kiss filled with the longing that had built up between them, the promise of a new beginning. When they parted, Mala's eyes were alight with a coy smile, and Chandra too couldn't help but smile. "It took time," she whispered, "but it was worth it."

Chapter 14: The Beginning

68

Ambika was sitting on the veranda enjoying the cool breeze when one of her neighbours approached her. A woman from the neighbouring house, asked her about her daughters-in-law, "Do they still fight like before? They used to fight all the time."

Ambika chuckled and replied, "No, not anymore. From the day I locked them in a room together, they have been inseparable. They sit together, eat together, sleep together, and even take baths together. It's almost like they have become the best of friends."

The neighbour woman was surprised and asked, "Really? That's quite strange. I've never heard of such a thing."

Ambika nodded, "Yes, it is strange. But I'm not complaining. It's such a relief to have peace in the house. And, they both look so happy and content."

The two women laughed and shared a few more stories about their respective families. The conversation lightened up their mood of Ambika felt grateful for the small things in life that bring so much joy and happiness.

Ambika thought to herself, who would have thought that two women who were once enemies, would come together and form such a strong bond. It was truly a miracle and a testament to the power of love and forgiveness.

69

As Chandra combed Mala's hair, she leaned into her touch, feeling the tenderness and love that was always present between them. The two women sat on the floor, surrounded by the warmth of their love for each other, as Chandra gently placed a kiss on Mala's cheek. She then took out the chain with the crescent moon pendant, the same pendant that was on her own neck, and fastened it around Mala's neck. The two chains, identical in every way, shone around the necks of both women, a symbol of their love for each other.

As they looked at each other, their eyes met and a smile spread across their faces, as though they were the only two people in the world. At that moment, all the hardships, the pain and the fear faded away, leaving only the love they had for each other. Their son Bhagia, who was playing on the floor with a bunch of wildflowers, adding to their happiness and contentment.

The room was filled with love and warmth, as the two women basked in the joy of their love for each other. They had been through so much together, but their love had only grown stronger, cementing their bond as if nothing could come between them.

Chandra took Mala's hand and whispered, "I love you, my beautiful. You complete me in every way and I promise to love you for all of my life."

Mala, with tears in her eyes, replied, "I love you too, my darling. You are my everything and I am so grateful for your love and for being by my side every step of the way."

As they held each other close, the room was filled with

the sound of Bhagia's laughter, the fluttering of the wildflowers, and the beating of two hearts, intertwined forever. They were basking on their love story, a story of two women who had found each other in the most unexpected of places and had held onto each other through every trial and tribulation; they were proud of their love that was unbreakable, unyielding, and as strong as the chains around their necks.

***